The Economist

Christopher Grimes

SPUYTEN DUYVIL
New York City

© 2022 Christopher Grimes
ISBN 978-1-956005-44-8

Library of Congress Cataloging-in-Publication Data

Names: Grimes, Christopher, author.
Title: The economist / Christopher Grimes.
Description: New York City : Spuyten Duyvil, [2022] |
Identifiers: LCCN 2022012958 | ISBN 9781956005448 (paperback)
Subjects: LCGFT: Novels.
Classification: LCC PS3607.R556 E27 2022 | DDC 813/.6--dc23/eng/20220317
LC record available at https://lccn.loc.gov/2022012958

for Sofie

CONTENTS

The Preface

The Note on Method

Vol I: The Field of Play

Vol II: Getting Back on Track

Wherein the foundational argument is summarized, namely that the former Trump administration's focus on the US/Mexico border ignored the mounting anxieties of untold numbers of American individuals and businesses alike occupying the US/Canadian border. In other words, a return to a greater America was not ultimately achievable because, along with economic issues to be discussed in detail momentarily, the convection caused by the "hot winds" (Maddick) remained unacknowledged, especially with regard to how they will eventually render the deep south a par-baked irrelevancy. The increasingly temperate northern border with Canada will, as a result, become the site of much sociological, political, environmental, personal and economic upheaval, as entirely unavoidable as the abstractions deployed here to describe them, necessitated by the otherwise almost unspeakable catastrophe they try to approximate. Like the processes involved in hydraulic fracturing—itself a subsidiary concern of the present work—the general lay of the land needs to be surveyed before drilling down.

That said, a brief expression of gratitude to the members of the Economic Coalition of North Dakota (ECOND), Freyman Municipal Chapter, for all those countless, heated conversations that, after the streets were plowed and the hats and gloves hung to dry, went well into the night, until, as so often happened, the manager of the Applebee's on RR 59—situated directly across the road from the Divide County Clinic (to be featured elsewhere), the Flying J truck stop and Motel 6, altogether forming a kind of bright, welcoming oasis in an otherwise Midwestern frigid, winter night—was compelled to "clear the booth," announcing that it was past closing time, thus scattering the coalition, now broken into its constituent parts, stumbling onto the salted parking lot and its amber, phosphorescent glow, the falling snow appearing like flakes of gold.

These social interactions were halted, of course, due to the Covid-19 pandemic, the abatement measures of which remain at present so politically controversial (i.e., "social distancing," "masking") and situationally fluid that it (the pandemic) will occupy as little space as possible here. Fortunately, at the time of this writing help is on the horizon, courtesy of our bio-pharmacological research infrastructure (the Pfizer vaccine, the Moderna vaccine, et al.). Suffice it to say that any solitary researcher, anxious introvert or clinical depressive could rightly welcome us into this world, even act as a sort of tour guide, or provide tips as to how to inhabit this sudden, as Roland so interestingly (and surprisingly) put it in his thoughts on economic projections and pandemics (2021), this "physical manifestation of mind," its echoey isolation so foreign to the newly arrived. So here, then, should be a sort of PSA to buoy the mood by way of a rallying cry around the notion that the anecdote of despair is engagement. An encouragement to shake off the panicked paralysis, cut the Klonopin in half, and deploy whatever skills that might lay dormant in order to claim some measure of agency.

In conclusion, a brief history of socio-political-economic conditions around the globe, with particular emphasis on 1) America, and 2) Canada.

A Note on Method

A following "in flight" behind such historically neglected contributors to the field of economics as Bronislaw Malinowski—read, for example, the "account of native enterprises," as captured in his *Argonauts of the Western Pacific* (1922), speaking of the middle of nowhere—and his edict to "jump off the veranda," as he put it, into "it" (native culture), in order to observe, to get on with it, to mix it up and talk to some mature adults for a change, to take a good look at all the stuff strewn about here (even the desiccated dog droppings to be considered, given the voluble Curbing Law debate happening across the US, which weighs the increase of plastic dog waste bags in community landfills against "natural composting") and over there (a plastic VW hubcap), to consume the local foods (Canada's cuisine to be leered at elsewhere), to have a drink with the grownups, to, in short, *go native* (the phrase apparently coined by Samuel de Champlain to describe Etienne Bruel, after he—Bruel—was dismembered and eaten by the Hurons, who believed him a Iroquois spy). A reminder now that the obligatory turn toward Indigenous Peoples and their issues must be taken up, at least at some point later on.

Also, a more explicit claim that, as the adoption of Bronislaw Malinowski's methodology suggests, the study of economics today is thought to borrow a good deal from the ethnographic disciplines: think Malinowski transported into innumerable American homes, sitting at the kitchen table, drinking a tepid Folgers and eating a sprouted grain toast while simultaneously balancing a checkbook and transcribing a dictated grocery list. The lighting, LED meant to approximate the amber glow of incandescence.

Here he (Malinowski) is, *watching*, his intense stare perched above the malleable nose piece of his N-95 surgical mask. He brushes dandruff flakes off the shoulders of his black, cable-knit turtleneck sweater onto the kitchen floor, precisely when no one's looking, in an effort not to call attention to himself. And then he's off to explore a world that is perpetually new to him, foreign, unique.

He'd see the 140 milliliter plastic bottles of Sutter Home Cabernet Sauvignon rolling around the floor of a truck's cab in a completely novel context, wherein they might appear to him as rare and precious artifacts, something that might be delicately consumed on an outbound transatlantic flight already far above and away from here.

A turn now back to the matter at hand by way of a few facts meant to bolster some of the methodological points made above, mainly that the American Economic Association's most recent iteration of what economists actually *do* is, one might say, "trenchantly anthropological in scope." How, the Association asks, do human beings respond to scarcity and how do they use their resources? what decisions do American families in particular make—it's the *American* Economic Association, after all—in any given situation, and *why*? This is the obvious trend line, pointing to a profession leaning towards an opinion that in order to understand better a general condition (i.e., macro-conditions), there must be a willingness to study the discreet, often culturally produced particulars (i.e., micro-conditions) that cohere to give rise to generalities.

The level of attention and scrutiny of the project at hand will require, therefore, to borrow from military terminology, "embedding," as when a journalist is said to be "embedded" with the unit he or she is reporting on in a combat zone.

That said, here then is the plan for the present work:

Volume 1:
The Field of Play

1.1/1)   an introductory survey of the coronavirus pandemic's impact on the US's gross domestic product—to date, a "staggering" (*Forbes*) 31.4 %—and unemployment, which is at 14.7% and rising, as opposed to Canada's positive growth in the same indices, with a 2% increase in GDP and -1% number of unemployed, in other words an *increase* in over-employment (read: labor *shortage*), which well and truly lays bare the inequities and of health care and income distribution between the two countries;

1.2/2) an acknowledgment that Canada's threat to the United States has already been well-documented in several more or less thoroughgoing works on the subject;

1.3/3) a specific reference to how R.M. Metclaff and Presten Eddy have adequately detailed the phenomena of "population drift," whereby retirement-aged Canadians have historically relocated to such perennial US retirement destinations as Georgia, the Dakotas and Florida, the latter state having the notorious distinction of producing such arcane and unenforceable child-support laws that men from both countries yearly migrate and eventually die on its shores like so much putrefying salmon after the spawn;

1.4/4) an abbreviated argument on how the current Canadian southbound drift will reverse itself, the flow returning northward;

1.5/5) brief comments on the US "professional class" —in other words, those US nationals who are by most accounts both materially and intellectually viable contributors to the public purse —and how they are increasingly attempting to migrate to Canadian cities (Vancouver, Toronto, Quebec, etc.), a demographic shift that, in the waning days of the 20th century and the opening days of the 21st, are attributable to earlier trends that include the conflict in Vietnam, followed by an ebb in the 1980s and 90s, followed again by a flow linked to the advent of the second (H.W.) Bush and recent Trump administrations;

1.6/6) evidence that shows how the effect of migration has arguably created a "brain drain" (Eddy) in the US, with the simultaneous disadvantage of Americans having to fund human services for the typical as-of-now remaining Canadian ex-pats (see "Resident Aliens"), overwhelmingly inclined as they are toward myriad and therefore costly geriatric afflictions, rendering a large number of them not only in-ambulatory, but very nearly wards of the Welfare State;

1.7/7) evidence that shows the relationship between the United States and Canada increasingly evincing a strict inequality (expressed by the following formula: $U < C$, where U = USA and C = Canada), resulting in an increasingly familiar scenario that finds a US head of household not only supporting her own direct dependents, but also having to financially support a failing Canadian parent (aka., "Resident Alien," "in-law," "mother," "grandmother," etc., etc.), representing yet another dying body thrown at America's feet;

1.8/8) a more general and sweeping introduction to the innumerable number of Resident Aliens living Stateside here to take advantage of various medical interventions (i.e., bariatric procedures, joint replacements) not *immediately* available (but available nonetheless, given enough time and a little patience) by Canada's socialized medical system, however highly praised by the otherwise medically indigent Resident Aliens as they "wear the shine off our country's dining room floor" (Metclaff) in their sleek Zip'r Roos, themselves made in the USA and potentially subsidized, at least in part, by US taxpayer supported Medicare;

1.9/9) a footnote directing one to a logically predictable, though somewhat artless spreadsheet produced by the US State Department titled "Resident Aliens of Canadian National Origin by State." As so often happens, utility alone determines such choices;

1.10/10) a comparison of confirmed Covid-19 cases in Canada (pop. 37.59 million) and the US (pop. 328.2 million): 579K cases with 15,590 deaths, as opposed to 19.8 million cases with 343K deaths, respectively (Dec., 2020). Percentages to population to be figured;

1.11/11) a little something to cheer things up. Something that maybe works like marigolds in the springtime. An admission, meanwhile, to a little more snow;

A Visit to the Borderlands

2.1/12) a more detailed description of the worrisome "drain" caused by the inequitable "drift" at the heart of the US economy (literally "draining" some of it off). Such effects, like the way bad circulation is initially felt in the numbing of the little toe, are first manifest in the periphery, the small townships located at the extremities of the country, these hamlets on the border, these barely habitable berms thrown up against the cold and dark frontier, where nevertheless the growing discrepancy in "quality of life indicators" (Samuelson) are abundantly evident by comparing two border communities—Freyman, ND (USA) and Estevan, SK (Canada)—which are separated by one and a half miles and the absolute fullness of two countries;

2.2/13) comparables of so-called "soft" census data represented by the following squat Pareto graph, flannel grey grid with navy blue bars indicating the US, and garnet red bars indicating Canada. Numeric indices left justified in Palatino Linotype:

Indicator	Freyman, ND	Estevan, SK
Population	139	11,135
Population change since 2000	-9.7%	-1.4%
Median resident age	58.0	37.5

For population 25 yrs and over

College degree/Trade Cert.	4.7%	35%

For population 15 yrs and over

Never married	11.5%	31%
Now married	56.8%	53%
Separated	1%	2%
Divorced	20%	6%
Median household income	$28,677 (USD)	$80,710 (USD)
Most common industries	Waste Management & Health Care	Sales and Service & Trade
Median home value	$16,678 (USD)	$153,808 (USD)
Motto	N/A	Sunshine Capital of Saskatchewan

2.3/14) the observation that these two towns in two distinct countries are stretched out side by side like some long married couple, always touching, yet ultimately closed off to one another, absorbed, as they are, in the separate preoccupations teaming within their respective borders, their separate skins, their many states;

2.4/15) how borders themselves might represent the infinitely reducible distinction between "You" and "I," both married, in other words, and somehow unmarried to each other. But what if the width of a border, whatever that width might be, is halved? And that half halved again, and then halved again and again and again? At what point is it no longer possible to say "come to me," but instead "enter into me, just as I am entering into you?";

2.5/16) a list of possibilities that might arise from a complete comingling on this unstable marker between all that destruction required for becoming a *one*. The doubled resources, ambitions, dreams and hopes brought into a something of a singular thing;

2.6/17) the possibility that to know oneself fully might be to fully know two. Is it here that all the anxieties produced by the separation might evaporate like some stupid argument, like whose turn is to walk the dog or do the dishes, or who, in the past, was going to take who to music lessons at 6:30, what's the cost/benefits of probiotic "supplements," who's going to roll the Resident Alien over and outfit her with a fresh pair of Depends now that the wife is self-quarantining at the clinic, sleeping on one of the cots donated from the North Dakota National Guard after the Turtle Mountain Reservation outbreak in September, and who, despite the fact that the daughter of the Resident Alien is a practicing *family* physician—someone therefore presumably skilled and learned in the ways of treating an *entire* family, from the very youngest to the very oldest—will apply the Terrasil ointment to her bedsores now that that the rolling over is complete?;

2.7/18) by way of example of ever-mounting disparities, the as yet to be determined cost a Canadian national versus the cost an American national might spend for .5 milligrams of Clonazepam and 150 milligrams of Wellbutrin, constituting the typical titrating dose, taken daily;

Chpt 3:
Paying Attention

3.1/19) informed speculation which attempts to explain America's seeming refusal to pay attention to Canada's increasingly, if not economically *predatory*, then at least economically *suspicious* behavior, and how that lack of attention can be understood in a broader context;

3.2/20) Herbert Simon's quote that "What information consumes is rather obvious: it consumes the attention of its recipients";

3.3/21) Herbert Simon's quote that "A wealth of information creates a poverty of attention and a need to allocate that attention efficiently among the overabundance of information sources that might consume it." Thus attention becomes conceptually familiar as a resource in the economic principle of "resource scarcity" (in other words, in the discipline of economics itself);

3.4/22) proof of how attention spans have fallen from 12 seconds to 8 seconds in the last 15 years;

3.5/23) a question: where is the increasingly precious and rare commodity of attention spent? The data, compiled from 2008 to 2015 (Venrock), in the form of a stacked Cartesian graph, the border representing 2008's data set in pink, the border representing 2015's data set in a sickly taupe:

	2008	2015
TV	44%	36%
Digital computer (desktop or laptop)	23%	20%
Digital mobile device	3%	24%
Print media	11%	3%
Radio	18%	12%
Other (game consoles, etc)	2%	4%

3.6/24) the inescapable conclusion that the surge in attention-grabbing smart phones and tablets (a 21% increase in 7 years) is at the expense of television (which saw an 8% decrease) and print media (which also saw an 8% reduction, now commanding only a dismal 3% of our attention). A casual observation that the experience of quarantine has exponentially exacerbated these numbers in ways heretofore unknown;

3.7/25) the subsequent, and subsequently germane, recollection of a recent opinion piece, wherein its author laments sitting across the kitchen table from his wife, how she doesn't look at him, nor, even, at their child, but how she is instead immersed in the illuminated, entirely insular universe there in the palm of her hand. Its author's lament: that he and his family inhabit the same spaces so seldomly these days, what with their harried work and school schedules, so that he finds himself choking down the urge to slap that phone from her hand, to allow for the shock and pause, then the sharp sound of shattering glass and cracking circuitry (or whatever sound it is that a smart phone makes in its destruction,) all the while pleading "Pay attention to me! Pay attention to me! Pay attention to me!";

3.8/26) the admission that no one is immune to the tension caused by too little attention in a sea of information and distractions, including, for example, several rounds of Texas Hold'Em on a World Series of Poker app., processing a PayPal payment for on-line music lessons, using the facilities, doing a load of laundry, going on a "poop patrol" in the back yard, drinking a beer, briefly working on a plan to get out of all this, watching a super creepy YouTube video of a *Teletubbies* episode washed of color and set to Joy Division's "Atmosphere," checking email (x5), browsing Facebook, eating a pickle, making beds;

3.9/27) a retreat back to the obvious, that the attention economy is based on consumer products that cost nearly nothing, that attention itself is the most valuable resource on the field, and it is increasingly monetized;

3.10/28) the proposition that, as the digital culture theorist Kevin Kelly has pointed out, just getting one's attention requires a slew of "valuable intangibles," including immediacy (as in, "Here I am!"), personalization (as in, "How are you doing, by the way? What's on *your* mind?"), interpretation (see some planned stuff forthcoming about the Little Caesars Stadium, rising stars and settings suns), authenticity (as in, "This is the real deal."), accessibility (see "immediacy" above), embodiment (as in, "What's this all about?"), patronage (as in, "Thanks for being here!"), and, finally, find-ability (see "accessibility" above);

3.11/29) a graph now of survey results indicating just how lit-tle Americans know, or even think, about Canada? Or would this be counted as just so much clutter, what attention econ-omists define as information "pollution?" Would this provide an opportunity to draw direct parallels between the polluting of our attention, via such modalities as spam and other forms of advertising, and the polluting of our environment, via such modalities as the hydraulic fracturing industry and internal combustion?;

4.1/30) a summary of Canada's response to attention pollution—the Canadian Anti-Spam Legislation (CASL)—which is one of the most stringent laws of its kind in the world, requiring that all commercial electronic messages (that is, communications connected to commercial activity) have implied or explicit consent by the receiver before being sent;

4.2/31) speculation as to how CASL might be viewed as an especially onerous impediment (given its definition as an "excessively harsh and severe" set of laws, some might say *draconian*) to both free trade and the free exchange of ideas. In fact, such obviously counter-productive constraints are viewed as particularly puzzling to American citizens, who have a long tradition of valuing their First Amendment Rights (it hardly needs be said that Canadian citizens, of course, aren't able to similarly enjoy the First Amendment, inasmuch as their constitution is entirely different);

4.3/32) examples as to how the American capital market has posited several solutions to begin to "clean up" the suddenly and "catastrophically polluted superfund sites of our headspace" (Pritcher), including "interruption rights" (Fahlman), whereby a fee is attached to the demand on someone's attention, one that would be on a sliding scale,

with a CEO of a multi-national corporation being excessively expensive, for example, and an eighth grader with
a cell phone being nearly free. Fees would also increase
during peak times—birthdays, 9am to 5pm, and general
holidays—and decrease during low demand times: August,
midnight;

4.4/33) Loder, Van Alstyne and Wash floating the notion of
"attention bonds," whereby funds are put into escrow by
the sender of a message as a hedge (or "guarantee") that this
material is worthy of consideration, and not just a complete
waste of time;

 4.5/34) a total manifestation of the attention-tension dy-
namic as evidenced in a typical 13 year old American (one
eighth grader mentioned above, for example) , who, by
turns cheerful and full of energy—*ebullient*, in a word—
and morose, announces, to give but a few examples, that
homework is a waste of her time and attention, that school
itself is a waste of her time and attention, that even watching commercial TV is a waste of her time and attention.
Worthy of her attention: her musical recorder, to which her
parents (minus a mother of late) are her one and only re-
ceptive audience, as well as her dog, a puppy growing into
adolescence, who she also deems worthy of her time and
attention, at least sometimes. Also an apparently good use
of her time: sitting quietly at her dying, unreceptive grandmother's side, staring into the space occupied by that mostly supine, though occasionally prone, perceptibly respiring
form;

4.6/35) a brief elaboration on the subject of the aforementioned instrument, the recorder, which attempts to disclose all of its intentions, the entirety of its decision making apparatus (e.g., the girl herself) engaged in the mechanics of its own consumption of duration, becoming both defined and undefined simultaneously in the kitchen, consuming silence and attention in the living room, in the bedrooms (occasionally even in the dying grandmother's bedroom), in the bathroom and basement and all over the small, ranch-style home located in the heart of the town in which she lives;

4.7/36) some contemplation on the passage of time and attention, accompanied for the purposes of economy and compression by the following selections: 1) *Frere Jacques* (composer unknown) for the recorder, 2) Ludwig Van Beethoven's *Ode to Joy* for the recorder, 3) Benjamin Britten's *The Alpine Suite* for the recorder, complete with its six constituent parts, including the supposedly wonderment-inducing "Arrival at Zermatt," the supposedly romantic and mechanistic "Swiss Clock," the stutter steps and unsure footing apparently evoked in "Nursery Slopes," the supposed majesty of the "Alpine Scene," the *descending*, in other words *falling* notes of "*Moto Perpetuo*: Down the Piste," and, a "devastating nostalgia" (Schuller) already setting in, the "Farewell to Zermatt." And finally 4) a nod to the aspirational in the form of Vittorio Monti's sorrowful *Czardas* for the recorder, with piano accompaniment;

4.8/37) a qualifier that the word "supposedly" deployed above is meant as some kind of linkage to Canada's CASL addressed at the beginning of this chapter, probably something having to do with how CASL's constraint are similar to the infernal musical recorder itself, the harmonic range of which is so ultimately thin and flat as to render any composition an expression of ambivalence at best, at worst sheer annoyance;

4.9/38) a cataloging of the paucity of resources that the recorder itself represents, including inaccessibility to musical instruments with more emotional range, and how it therefore represents limited access to cultural resources and musical instruction, so that even the acrylic reproduction of the "Gottingen Recorder" (circa 1246-1322, original in fruitwood) discovered in the archeological excavation of a medieval latrine in Gottingen, Germany, is rendered inferior, because, as research after the fact of the purchase revealed, "its ancient, inflexible pitch resonates somewhere between soprano and alto, thus making it incapable of harmonizing" (Werner) with any of the three other recorders rolled up in a carrier that resembles a professional chef's knife kit;

4.10/39) the precious "Gottingen Recorder" reproduction ($439.99 USD on Amazon.com) shown to be incapable in fact of harmonizing with any modern recorder in any contemporary recorder context, a trio or even a simple duet, for example, anywhere in the entire world;

4.11/40) the necessity of repetition: the precious "Gottingen Recorder" reproduction shown to be incapable of harmonizing with any modern recorder in any contemporary recorder context, which the grandmother, when she was still able to speak, announced as a testament to her granddaughter's "old soul";

(4.12/41) a threat that if the recorder player doesn't stop playing "the Gottingen" for, like, one second, and instead turn on her Zoom camera and pay attention to her virtual algebra class, that she'll be good and grounded, to which a Bronislaw Malinowski would record her response, verbatim: "Jesus, dad, what're you going to do, keep me from 'seeing' my friends?" A marginal note that the word "seeing" is in air quotes;

CHPT 5:
THE CANADIAN INVASION

5.1/42) a sort of thought experiment, an example of the process by which one becomes a Resident Alien in the first place, an illustration how close Canadian and American economies have been, at least historically;

5.2/43) a "jumping off the veranda" smack into a summary of a not altogether atypical scene where a family member is sitting vigil for the doctor's dying mother, in this case maybe just lingering in the darkness for the moment, in the so-called dying light, with another family member, who, simultaneously morose and ebullient, glares into her grandmother's face while moving her own lips, always, as if she (the granddaughter) is about to say something, while maybe swabbing her grandmother's lips with glycerin or plumping her pillow (aka, "palliative care");

5.3/44) an opportunity that presents itself in silence to show exactly how she, the doctor's mother, arrived here in the first place, bathed now in the Technicolor light of the Hallmark Channel broadcasting on the little television set upon the dresser, the smell of burnt pizza hanging in the air. Just who burnt a pizza in the first place? In reply, Vivaldi's *Springtime* concerto adapted for the recorder;

5.4/45) a more general introduction to the concept of a "birth tourist" by way of a pregnant Canadian (the presently dying grandmother, the conspicuously missing doctor's mother) who arrived in the United States in 1981 at a motel/campground complex on the Northern Wisconsin side of the Boundary Waters. This arrival coinciding with the decade-long period which even the "Canadian Economics" entry in the *Canadian Encyclopedia* describes as "plagued by stagnation";

5.5/46) a recollection of that year—when the Resident Alien was still capable of recall—that, in Canada at least, *things were really crap.* Like most of her country people, she stuck her head up, took a look around, and gave her pronouncement of the general economic mood. But beneath her layperson's assessment were the following dire facts: dramatic increases in unemployment and inflation fueled by an abrupt slowdown in the rate of growth of real output and productivity;

5.6/47) emphasis on the word "dramatic," as one need only to take note of an 11.3% unemployment rate. From 1981 through 1983 alone, business capital spending fell a full 20%;

5.7/48) a black and white Control Chart (or Line Graph), whose soaring peaks and plummeting valleys depict Canadian GDP and consumer confidence, weirdly resembling, it's been remarked elsewhere, the electrocardiogram read-out of someone in pulseless ventricular tachycardia that usually precedes the "flatline" of asystole, the absence of ventricular contractions in the heart of the Canadian economy at that time;

5.8/49) the presentation of a vicious paradox, in that the pregnant Canadian couldn't have known as she stood there initially eyeing the US/Canadian border that she herself was a significant part of Canada's economic problems. More specifically, she was among the unprecedented number of women entering the work force—in other words, she and her baby-boomer sisters had flooded the labor market—all of whom contributed to intense competition for jobs in their native country, which in turn drove up the number of those who couldn't secure one. There was also a lingering wariness caused by the international oil price increase from 1972-1973. Then international oil price increased *again* from 1979-1980. But there was a path to a better future. If not directly for the mother, then at least for her baby;

5.9/50) recognition that this same scenario—the same decision making processes—was playing out by the thousands, if not tens of thousands, if not possibly hundreds of thousands of times. And by "decision making processes," what's being referred to here are "women themselves": women's brains, women's bodies, their hair, their faces, the way they behave, the babies growing in their wombs (or not), their sum totality. *Etcetera*;

5.10/51) a question of where the father is lurking in all of this. Perhaps soaking up the sun on some beach in Florida, drinking a cold Coors Light, surreptitiously pissing in the condo's pool instead of taking care of his wife and soon-to-be kid. Whatever. Given the dire state of the Canadian economy in the late 1970s and early 1980s, it's small wonder that so many women, alone or not, "dropped down from the north like bad weather" (Bannon) to take advantage of the US's unconditional birthright citizenship, its policy of *jus soli* ("right of the soil") protected by the Fourteenth Amendment;

5.11/52) further explanation of the policy that by giving birth to her child in the US, the child herself would be afforded all the benefits of American citizenship, not the least of which would be an American passport, "free" K through 12 public education and the possibility of in-state tuition at an American college after secondary school;

5.12/53) an updating of these series of maneuvers into current parlance, the setting of an "anchor baby," with the implication that the child could one day sponsor her own mother (and the father?) should they too decide to immigrate and apply for US citizenship. But this summary represents only half the story and will therefore need to be split into two;

6.1/54) the baby girl, who would one day become the doctor—the doctor currently quarantined in the clinic, literally surrounded by a horde of desperately sick Indians (see the Turtle Mountain Reservation outbreak earlier) and their contagion—is birthed;

6.2/55) the mother's and baby's return to Canada. Some twenty years later, just as predicted, the now-legal adult daughter arrives back in the United States of America to take up residency in Wisconsin for the purpose of attending two University of Wisconsin schools, earning a Bachelor of Science at UW-Milwaukee, where she would meet her future husband (who himself would never complete his degree in International Finance, for reasons that should probably be explained a little later), then completing her MD at UW-Madison;

6.3/56) an admission that this summary might be seen as little more than a series of tedious data points, but it's imperative for setting up the context of what's sure to be read as a "breathlessly ironic" (re-read Kathleen Parker's "Opinions" piece in the April 17, 2020, edition of *The Washington Post*) reversal of fortunes, set to something like A.V. Alexandrov's "National Anthem of Russia" for the recorder;

6.4/57) as previously intimated, a pause to briefly introduce the aforementioned soon-to-be, at this time, husband, whose own economic backstory might make him a sort of early 21st century Everyman: the dropping out of his Finance program to be swept up in the housing boom, not only because there was so much money to be made, but also for the adventure of it. The two years on a crew that built track housing in the South from Atlanta to Arkansas. The fact that he's *good* at it, so by 2006 he's slipped into sales and a six-figure salary. In fact, based on his adjusted gross annual income, as an income chart could verify, he's able to secure the necessary loans for his fiancé's medical school. But the next year the bottom falls out of the American housing market. Unemployment above 10%, with those employed in housing disproportionately affected. As the saying goes, "that's the end of that" (anonymous);

6.5/58) the introduction of a concurrent event at the time: the conception of their own child, the recorder impresario playing the Russian National Anthem, the doctor's daughter, the grandmother's granddaughter, just to be clear. Another fourteen years later, and here they are, economically stranded in the wild west of the fracking boom, surrounded on all sides by the shudder of downshifting diesel engines at all hours of the day and night. The mother, a practicing physician, the father a kind of jack-of-all-trades, dabbling in a little bit of everything, from rebooting a Wifi modem to raising a kid to general handyman projects. Plows snow for the Freyman Township in the winter, does private plowing on the side. Mows grass for Freyman Township in the summer, does private mowing on the side. Not exactly what he's so-called "trained" for, not the biggest return on his "investment," so to speak, but it is what it is;

6.6/59) the introduction of the Canadian mother's relatively recent diagnosis of Acute Lymphoblastic Leukemia. But rather than take advantage of the aforementioned socialized medical system available in her home country, she accepts her daughter's invitation to "do hospice" in the US, and, thus, not die alone. So while her daughter wears herself thin at the rural clinic, her mother is quietly disassembling toward absolute incoherence in the guest room, from which a pall now emanates across the hallway floor outside her door, flickering colors from her little television, which always seems to be on, and in the background, the tinny notes of a recorder, always playing, playing, playing, like the unnerving tone television stations used to emit after the evening's programming ended and the station went off the air;

6.7/60) the claim that one could be forgiven from reading a message into it, that light. What's to be learned from it? Who knows, but that the American family's palliative efforts amount to a vigil around an idea that doesn't factually exist, or doesn't exist any longer. And still they embrace her, like embracing the shed exoskeleton of a cicada, arrested in its stillness. All empty, empty;

6.8/61) an opportunity here to dispel a number of cliques depicting the "typical Canadian" as bonneted, Rubenesque, apple-cheeked prairie maidens or plaid shirted, thin-lipped lumberjacks, and instead consider the recent (2009) likening of Canada to an effeminate male—"thin wristed," "soft spoken," "smelling of soap," "as adept with information technologies as it [Canada] is with a pneumatic nail gun" (Weber);

7.1/62) a dropping down into the site-specific example of Freyman itself, as if, to follow Malinowski's lead, for the very first time. A stroll through its streets on a Sunday back in early December, alkali aroma of snow in the air (the first whiffs of "white gold," at least for those employed by NDOT, who will be earning overtime to plow it, as stipulated by the latest State contract), the sky the color of graphite, a kind of leaden daylight, mostly free of exhaust particulates—it being a Sunday, the least amount of traffic of the entire week—so there's little bending of the daylight's photons, and contrasts therefore appear more vivid, as opposed to a weekday, when geometric patterns seem to grow a sort of fuzz, sharp edges a little blurred by the pollution;

7.2/63) the inclusion of a side note for emphasis: on a Sunday the traffic tally is comparatively light at the Freyman-Estevan Border Crossing;

7.3/64) the appearance of the occasional "big rigs" heading west, and now the water tanker operated by Standard Oil-Canada, which comes through town twice daily, seven days a week, en route from some water purification source in Saskatchewan to Clydesville, ND (and then back again), in compliance with an international court order to provide, indefinitely, Clydesville with its potable water, representing just one of several legal remedies resulting from Standard Oil-Canada's thoroughly trashing Clydesville's aquifer. As the presiding judge determined, which she herself put into the following layman's terms in her final ruling: "kiss Clydesville goodbye";

7.4/65) the dropping in of this interestingly little factoid, especially given the Turtle Mountain Reservation's proximity to Clydesville (6 miles northwest), the Turtle Mountain Tribe was the first to successfully oppose hydraulic fracturing on their lands in North America;

7.5/66) back to Freyman itself, and a harrowing climb to the top of one of the two grain elevators on Main Street to make a survey. Down below, the Speak Easy Bar, the bordered-up edifice of the Wayfarer's Hotel, St. Patrick's Catholic Church, the State Bank, the Piggly Wiggly supermarket, the Paradise Lutheran Church, the Roughneck Bunkhouse (within which is the Primaro Mexican Restaurant), the Zion Church, another grain elevator looming in the distance;

7.6/67) a bird's eye view of the U-shape of the Divide County Clinic off Route 59 West toward Anders, and, just a mile and a half northward, where Freyman's and Estevan's town lines meet, Canada itself;

7.7/68) this description of the houses down below: lots of double-wide trailers improved upon to create the effect of modest little homes. And there's streets, of course, mostly empty—it being Sunday, the day of rest. The relative quiet of this moment is a reminder of the certainty that itinerate traffic will begin around 4 am;

7.8/69) the absolute certainty that by breakfast, there'll be full-blown congestion to the point of near gridlock, a vehicular coagulation in the heart of Freyman. Semi and semi-trailers, many hundreds of them throughout the day, carrying the constituent parts that will be assembled upon on innumerable fracking pads erected across the Bakken Shale Deposit;

7.9/70) the promise of even more trucks, transporting slurry blenders, high pressure pumps, fracturing fluid and proppant storage tanks, low pressure flexible hosing, various meters and gauges, well casings, cement, sand king mixers, wireline, pig launchers and receivers, untold numbers of valves, bits, manifolds, drilling motors, pressure vessels, you name it, and more tanker-trucks transporting methanol, isopropyl alcohol, 2-butoxyethonol, acetic acid, hydrochloric acid, citric acid, sodium chloride, sodium and potassium carbonate, polyacrylamide (aka, "slickwater"), glutaraldehyde, ethylene glycol, isopropanol, gaur gum, and various gels and lubricants. And even more trucks still, stacked up in the westbound lane, with occasional eastbound liners hauling out brine and flowback and sludge, as well as filter cake, filter socks and solid waste and drill cuttings (BakerHughes, Hailiburton, Schlumberger, Breitling Energy, STI, FA, et. al.);

7.10/71) a reiteration that come tomorrow a.m. this runty little town will absolutely stink of traffic, to the point that the municipal board has long since stopped trying to maintain the roads, so that Main has gone to pulverized rubble, all but impossible to plow;

7.11/72) the hard fact that it's not the trucks stopped and idling during peak traffic times that cause the most consternation, even as they pump so many metric tons of diesel exhaust straight into children's faces and down into their pink lungs. It's those drivers who barrel through town off-hours, at high speeds, in an effort to avoid the aforementioned delays. Main Street, 2 a.m., 45-50 miles per hour;

7.12/73) an appropriate re-referencing of the "quality of life indicators" provided earlier;

7.13/74) the recollection of the recent altercation between US and Canadian hockey fans at the Little Cesar's Stadium in Detroit, Michigan, which will be taken up in in the next chapter, and how it might be seen as instructive;

[Insert, plate 1: US Geological Survey satellite image of the region under consideration, depicting Kermit and Paulson townships to the west of Freyman, Freyman itself, Strange Siding and Larson townships to the east, and strip mines to the immediate south, all of it embedded in a vegetal background the color of mint-flavored Milk of Magnesia that progressively deepens in hue until it crosses the pine-green border between the US and Canada, on the other side of which lies Estevan, nestled just above the mouth of the aforementioned Boundary Dam Reservoir, itself (the reservoir) fed by Lake McDonald to the west; to the north, the Estevan Aerodrome and Moose Mountain Provincial Park; and, stretching eastward, Dauphin Lake, Lake St. Martin, Lake Winnipegosis, Swan Lake, Pelican Lake, Inland Lake, Cedar Lake, Red Deer Lake, Ebb and Flow Lake, Dog Lake, Mire Lake, Spence Lake, until these and other innumerable bodies of water simply fall off the right edge of the frame]

CHPT 8:
HOCKEY! OR A WAR OF THE MIDDLE CLASSES

8.1/75) a statement of the obvious: life before the pandemic, back in the "normal times" that everyone seems to be pining for, was not all that rosy. Consider, for example, the November 2019 fight that broke out in the parking lot of Little Caesars Stadium in Detroit, Michigan, after the Detroit Red Wings (5-2-0) beat the Toronto Maple Leafs (2-4-1) four to two. Upwards of over 350 people were involved, almost exclusively males (albeit of varying ages), who were roughly split between Maple Leafs and Red Wings fans. Such violence is deemed instructive when the innumerable economic stressors that created it are considered;

8.2/76) eyewitness reports—reports of those who saw the bodies at war, the teeth that were knocked out, the ripping of clothing on those bodies, their heavy-booted kicking—indicated that it was a small group of Red Wings fans that seem to have started the altercation, taunting Maple Leafs fans by calling them "skeletons," a common Leaf-specific insult referring to the state of the body of those who witnessed the awarding of the last Stanley Cup to Toronto (1967), and therefore just the latest linguistic jab in a long and rich lexicon of insults, as understood by anyone familiar with the rivalry;

8.3/77) a summary of the exchanging of blows, the butting of heads, the kicking of a downed man, the hollow thunk of unyielding instruments (ice scrapers, rolled up programs, hockey sticks, umbrella handles, even an Aveda Wooden Paddle Hairbrush reportedly wielded in the melee) on skulls;

8.4/78) corroborating reports indicating that the origin of the violence seemed to be an amplification of a relatively minor skirmish between a Red Wings defenseman and a Maple Leaf left-winger that had occurred earlier on the ice;

8.5/79) a question, again: why bring all this up, particularly when most sports fans don't even really care for hockey? Witness Nielson Rating data on *regular* sports viewership— averages exclusive of major tournaments, series, cups and bowls—made evident in the following petite quartiles table whose horizontal columns might follow an intermittent white and baby blue pattern:

Organization	Viewership
NFL	17,400,000
NASCAR	7,100,00
NBA	1,400,00
MLB	690,000
NHL	500,000
MLS	320,000*

8.6/80) *a note at the bottom of the graph above explaining that Major League Soccer's playoff season is included in order to show how statistically proximate the National Hockey League is to the floor of sports viewership;

8.7/81) a closer look at the "average" hockey fan and how it might well shed light on the real source of that night's violence: while the NBA boasts 45% Black viewers, and Major League Soccer has in excess of 34% Hispanic viewers, the National Hockey League's viewership is overwhelmingly Caucasian, coming in at 92%. Who are they? Who knows for sure? But as the previous graph indicates, there are at least a half a million of them, and yet as Nielsen only examines the viewing habits of US households, the entire Canadian contingent of fans is left out of the equation;

8.8/82) the statistic that Canadian fans of their national hockey teams that compete in the NHL—teams which include the Montreal Canadiens, Ottawa Senators, Winnipeg Jets, Edmonton Oilers, Calgary Flames, Vancouver Canucks, and of course, the Montreal Maple Leafs—is estimated at 14 million;

8.9/83) an economic backstory that begins to get interesting, but one that can only be fully appreciated when more data is considered—specifically average annual salaries of the *entirety* of the NHL fan base;

8.10/84) a summary of the annual salaries of the average hockey fan, both Canadian and American, presented as a stacked column chart in peach, sky, concord, cherry and vine, respectively:

Less than 20K per year   : 9%
20K-40K per year   : 12%
40K-75K per year   : 27%
75K-100K per year   : 20%
100K+ per year   : 33%;

8.11/85) a repetition of the assertion that NHL fans are, on average, the most wealthy fans of any professional sport in North America. And yet beneath the aggregate lurks some Truly Alarming Trends (TATs);

8.12/86) TATs uncovered by the Luxembourg Income Study Database, which recently revealed that Canada has surpassed the US for the mantel of richest middle class in the entire world;

8.13/87) in simple summary form, the statistic that the average American middle class family earns between (USD) $40,000 and $75,000 annually, with a forecast that suggests a continued stagnant trajectory, while the average Canadian middle class family brings in an estimated (USD) $86,000 annually, with a trajectory toward increase;

8.14/88) a deeper look into the economic profile of the approximately 14 million Canadian hockey fans, which reveals that 58% earn (USD) 100K-250K annually, live in Alberta (62%), vote Conservative (59%) and have children (58%). (Bozinoff);

8.15/89) a claim that the inequity only gets worse. Salary data indicates that the average US hockey fan actually ekes out an existence in those categories making less than (USD) 20K to less than 75K per year, while Canadian fans can brag that their average income category is more than (USD) 75K annually (generally much, much more);

8.16/90) additional reasons for the income disparity between US and Canadian wage earners, including the well-known, notorious subsidization strategy carried out by the Canadian government—its socialistic, single-payer medical care, significantly lower tuition, less income inequality in the distribution of corporate profit sharing, a higher minimum wage and lower mortgage rates—so that it doesn't take much to see how greatly disadvantaged the US middle class is when competing with its Canadian counterpart in the global market;

8.17/91) a suggestion that the violence between NHL fans that occurred at the Little Caesars Stadium in Detroit is therefore not without its symbolism. One could be forgiven for thinking of how Little Caesars brings to mind the fate of ancient Rome, of course. Or how members of the US middle class, like the Roman citizenry during the empire's twilight, suffers from what many behavioral economists describe as "aggrieved entitlement" (Kimmel), a condition born when citizens of Rome felt entitled to, but did not receive, what they expected due to them, and how the scourge of humiliation subsequently pervaded that land;

8.18/92) a question now, plain and simple: what does one do when one feels humiliated? when one's deprivations has left one feeling "economically emasculated" (Lucias)? In a fit of rage, perhaps, one projects it onto their perceived rival, those "skeletons," in an effort to emasculate *them*, and when that doesn't satisfactorily re-establish balance: attack. Attack hard and with abandon;

8.19/93) a reminder here to provide a detailed explanation of the motivating behavior(s) animating the "seditious mob " (Acosta) of Trump-supporting "patriots" (Carlson) "demonstrating" (is this the right term?) at the US Capital Building;

CHPT 9:
THE DIVIDE COUNTY CLINIC: A CASE STUDY

9.1/94) a crucial qualification to begin with, which is that this is an introduction to the clinic *before* the pandemic, when the clinic looked like what a clinic looks like. Bright and shiny. Some kids' stuff in the corner for the kids;

9.2/95) an introduction to what the clinic used to smell like, what a former Canadian PM describes as a "geriatric funk" ("Traveling south from Windsor to Detroit, there's an abrupt change in the atmosphere, as if falling down the stairs into a damp cellar, or suddenly finding yourself entering the olfactory funk of a geriatric ward..."), the unmistakable comingling of urine and feces and various astringents, most noticeably Pine-Sol;

9.3/96) an introduction also to the one full-time doctor at the clinic, a . . . *lithe* (i.e., "mild, calm, slim but not skinny, flexible, strong, limber," example: "the elephant's lithe proboscis") woman in her early-ish forties, complaining that she can't seem to scrub hard enough to get the smell off her (the geriatric funk), that it's in her pores, coating her sinus cavities, almost like a latex paint;

9.4/97) the unfortunate fact that the doctor brings the smell home with her—back when she came home—that her daughter announces that she, the doctor, really stinks, like for real, like *really*;

9.5/98) other witnesses confirming the doctor's reek. It's in her hair, in her clothes, on her pale, porcelain skin (asked to describe herself by the publisher of *The Local Shopper* who was doing a "feature" on her when she and her family first arrived, she replied, half-jokingly, but which some read as an attempt at some impressive posturing—or posturing to be read as impressive—"a recessive allele on the 16th chromosome that manufactures an altered version of the MC1R protein." A redhead, in other words. Funny!);

9.6/99) the observation that the doctor's patients historically fall broadly into two categories: geriatric and traumatic. As regards the latter, Freyman, like other small communities positioned on what's been dubbed the "Bakken Shale Trail" (those communities subject to—and, in some cases, finding themselves in the servicing of—the transportation of goods supporting in excess of thirty-seven oil companies engaged in hydraulic fracturing of the Bakken shale formation), has seen a 60% increase in auto-related injuries, asthma causally linked to the increase in aforementioned diesel exhaust from idling semis on Main Street, injuries related to drug and alcohol use as well as those caused by general violence;

9.7/100) the geographic reality that Freyman, unlike, say, Williston, is not well-positioned to be a service center for the industry (it's simply too far west of the Bakken Deposit), resulting in its mean population becoming both stagnant and aging, what economic demographers describe as a "death spiral." In other words, the town and its people are "aging out";

9.8/101) a generalization that the clinic's waiting room is either peopled with bewildered, nervous-looking octogenarians there to take their Alzheimer's Mini-Cog Tests, or boney, exhausted-looking men (mostly) who smell like cigarettes and stale beer, twitchy with caffeine and amphetamines, the back of their heads resting against the wall, grinding their teeth;

9.9/102) the question: why stay? Why not leave for greener pastures, as they say in this part of the country? The doctor's smart enough to be a doctor, but not smart enough find a better position? Really? A reason in three words: Students to Service Program (SSP). Our young(ish) doctor finds herself in—if not economic slavery *per se*—then economic servitude to the SSP, which accepts allopathic and osteopathic students in their last year of medical school and provides tuition and loan repayment assistance in exchange for working in a Health Professional Shortage Area (HPSA). In short, a deal with the devil;

9.10/103) an elaboration of the tradeoff existent in the SSP contract. In exchange for said "service," she and her husband and daughter are ordered off to a HPSA with "urgent need" (Freyman, to take the example at hand), one of thousands of fading pinpoints on the map. Here she will be awarded $120,000 in debt relief in exchange for at least 3 years of service (one and half of which are water under the bridge);

9.11/104) an obvious conclusion that the problem is debt, plain and simple, approximately $190,000 worth of it, hanging over the family like a piano in a silent comedy;

9.12/105) a reversion back to that "geriatric funk," and an admission that it doesn't help that it comes from both within and without the home. Witness the doctor's mother, the Resident Alien, dying in the family's guest room. Nor does it exactly add to the aromatherapy that the dog urinated on the doctor's favorite West Elm rug, that the dog defecated on the doctor's clean kitchen floor, when the dog, the ambient temperature having risen to an unseasonable 43 degrees in December in North Dakota, wasn't supposed to be in the in the house in the first place;

CHPT 10:
A DEATH, OF SORTS

10.1/106) a brief intersession in order to summarize a few other events occurring this past year, meaning that time immediately before the first reported cases of Covid-19 in the United States. Wasn't there already an unusual amount of death to be considered as…death, the beckoning "white light" (Dagnall, Drinkwater). A pause here to consider a chart illustrating that the closer one is to dying, the more, obviously, one consumes in terms of medical interventions and, if opted for, home health care. How does a nation and its people best confront it, the impending demise? The emphasis on palliative care offered by the European model does not suffice, for, like a teenage child, future-America hesitates at the threshold of the 49th parallel, nervously staring into the darkness of the room (is the dying dead yet?), not quite able to see the state of the matter at hand, but nevertheless able to abstract the general fact of *a* death, a gaze therefore informed by a sort of naive bewilderment at the motionless form of the living (if you can call dying living) before her. In such circumstances one tries to make good of what one can. To make the best of it, as the saying goes, something about double-negatives making a positive, a going on and on;

10.2/107) a snapshot of an American family contending with a grandmother's impending demise. Perhaps more charts and graphs to compare medical cost structures expended on hospice care, US v Canada. Simultaneously, reports that the family dog escaped out the entry door to the attached garage, and presumably then through the open garage door itself and on and on;

10.3/108) a sad fact. A sad fact that the dog's apparently run over. But this sad fact isn't immediately known so that the daughter (that is, the doctor's daughter)—who is developing every day into her mother's more definitive structures, clearly growing into a kind of scarily approximate image of her mother, white porcelain skin (though a little more freckled), red hair, lithe frame and all—could be seen around town within an hour of the dog's "escape" duct taping Xeroxed announcements in the Laundromat and on utility poles, alerting the public that "Velcro" was missing and promising a reward, complete with rectangular, hand-cut tabs on the bottom margin with phone number and $ sign and so on and so forth;

10.4/109) a summary of the daughter's return home, where her father led her into the very garage the dog was thought to have run away from, presenting to her Velcro's broken body wrapped tightly in an old, yellow sheet printed with faded flowers;

10.5/110) speculation on why the family named their dog Velcro in the first place. The dog's markings, white with black splotches, are said to have resembled a cow, in particular the Guernsey preferred by milk farmers in the region. The dog's hair—*hair*, not *fur*—grew in tight coils and bunches, almost Velcro-like to the touch. Given the hair texture, the vet's best guess upon initial examination: a mutt, with probably lots of poodle in it. And given the webbed paws and boxy snout and overall build, maybe some Labrador or Field Spaniel. Hell, maybe even some Portuguese Water Dog thrown into the mix, for all he knew. Though how a Portuguese Water Dog would end up in a rescue shelter in Bismarck, just about as far as one could get from either the East or West coastal water one can get, would be anybody's guess. That'd be a pretty rare and unusual breed to just be roaming around out there, especially in these parts;

10.6/111) the point that the anxiety surrounding Velcro's death was, for the father, a purposeful foreshadowing of the grandmother's immanent disappearance (truth be told, he'd confide, he's grateful for the distraction, as bad as that might sound), thus affording the father an opportunity to further prepare his daughter for *the* death, the big one, grandma's—presumably the more important and therefore more difficult death—through memorialization of the dog, something about a space left blank in in the heart the exact shape, weight and smell of Velcro, that goddamned dog. That's how it's going to be for grandma. That's presumably the point he was making with all this;

11.1/112) the introduction of transitional material, connoting the warping of space and time brought on by the SARS-CoV-2 virus, hatched from the distance shores of China, its taking hold in Europe, its arrival on the East and West Coasts of the United States, to, beginning in earnest this past fall, here, the Plain States, culminating in Chief of Staff, Wyoming Medical Center (Casper), Dr. Andy Dunn's declaring, "all of a sudden, it is 2:30 a.m., and you are holding a smartphone to let a husband say goodbye to his wife via FaceTime after 60 years of marriage" (Mamone);

11.2/113) an introduction to the name "Geronimo" Joe Jones, who was the first recorded death from Covid-19 at the Divide County Clinic. The same Geronimo Joe Jones of "Geronimo Joe's" at the intersection of Routes 5 and 42, the locally famous, ramshackle "restaurant" (takeaway or dining in—standing only—at the polyurethaned, plywood counter) frequented, typically in the summer, by families from Freyman and surrounding communities, and year-round by truckers on their way to the eastern edge of the Bakken Shale Deposit. Menu consisting of sloppy joe on Wonder Bread, choice of American cheese and/or fried yellow onions (as testament to his local fame, "sloppy joe" in fact colloquially known as "Geronimo Joe"). French fries fried in peanut oil. Bottled Sprite, Coke or Fanta in the serve-yourself upright. Absent a liquor license, cans of Miller or Miller Lite on the sly;

11.3/114) the rationale for focusing on Geronimo Joe, a singular, embodied illustration of certain high-risk underlying conditions, both economically and medically, that probably contributed to his own death and of those deaths in his community. A sort of collective obituary;

11.4/115) a detailed discussion of how five hurricanes in the Gulf of Mexico last summer and the tanking of the oil market due to quarantine, travel restrictions and various constraints on "doing business" resulted in oil being traded, for the first time in US history, at negative prices. Given plummeting consumption, there was simply nowhere to even store the surplus;

11.5/116) an attempt to picture the near-total suspension of hydraulic fracturing, the fracking pads unmanned, the well pumps quiet and unmoving, the enormous gravel parking lot surrounding Geronimo Joe's empty, prompting him to retreat back to his ancestral home in the Turtle Mountain Reservation and its peoples;

11.6/117) a closer look at Indigenous Peoples themselves, both at the Turtle Mountain Reservation specifically and among Northern Plains tribes in general, by way of mortality in comparison to the White, non-Hispanic population. A classic, Vertical Bar Chart in minimal black and white, statistics sourced from the *American Journal of Public Health*, the Center for American Progress, and Centers for Disease Control and Prevention. Heading: rate at which Indigenous Peoples die from the following conditions, compared to their White counterparts:

All causes of death	1.89 x more likely
Accidents	3.10 x more likely
Heart disease	1.58 x more likely
Cancer	1.51 x more likely
Diabetes	4.18 x more likely
Chronic liver disease	6.64 x more likely
Stroke	1.30 x more likely
Influenza & pneumonia	2.19 x more likely
Homicide	9.97 x more likely
Kidney disease	3.37 x more likely
Septicemia	3.25 x more likely
Suicide	2.62 x more likely
Hypertension	8.6 x more likely
Covid-19 mortality	1.8 x more likely

11.7/118) the reality that with all of the underlying conditions charted above, it's small wonder that the Divide County Clinic—the so-called healthcare network collaring the Turtle Mountain Reservation having become quickly overwhelmed—began seeing patients who presented with Covid-19 symptoms in greater and greater numbers. With one ventilator on premises and a nursing staff of only three, the clinic was quickly forced to transition into tri-age, until now it's a kind of macabre shipping terminal, a transom point to load the desperately ill human cargo into ambulances and medivacs headed to Bismarck and Fargo, or wherever that will admit them—nearly 40% lacking the most basic health insurance (Artiga, Arguello, Duckett)—and to send the less ill back home for a hopefully success-ful convalescence, the youngish doctor therefore more of a glorified shipping clerk than an MD at this point, quaran-tined in her shipping office, sucking in the sick air through a week old mask;

11.8/119) a small business owner in the area and therefore a de facto member of the Freyman Chapter of the Econom-ic Coalition of North Dakota, the common knowledge that Geronimo Joe himself suffered from no less than five of the co-morbidities outlined in the previously given graph, none of which —for the sake of privacy (and to avoid any hint of defamation)—will be disclosed here. It's commonly known, however, that the deceased had a deep thirst for what the old Westerns termed the "fire water," (Wayne), especially after his wife died some time ago, long before the pandemic, so that her death can be said to be totally unre-lated to the current crises;

11.9/120) a visit to the clinic grounds themselves, from which the doctor can be seen inside, pressed up against the brown smoked glass in order to be clearly viewed, slowly waving or blowing a kiss or giving a thumbs-up or just standing there, staring out, indistinct shadows and short flashes of color swirling behind her, as if inhabiting a deep pool full of fish in an otherwise fast moving river;

12.1/121) an inquiry into another population group within the site currently under consideration, which will add to a fuller understanding of the state of economic conditions operating within the site itself;

12.2/122) the deployment of a Bayesian Network Decision Graph (or "Influence Diagram") in gradations of gray, revealing some of the motivations fueling the relatively recent phenomena of the "stay at home dad" (SAHD), itself (the phenomena) acting as a kind of instrument-laden weather balloon in the US/Canadian economic atmospheres;

12.3/123) the revelation of some arguably radical shifts in "traditional" notions of who participates in the labor force, as well as what a family structure might look like on both sides of the border. This phenomena will furthermore show itself to be relatively recent. How so? Consider that in the 1970s six men in the entire United States claimed to be SAHD (Shifflett, Peck, Scheller). That's not 600,000 or 60,000 or even 6,000. It's six. Currently, an estimated 1.9 million men in the US identify as SAHD, making up roughly 16% of the entire stay-at-home-parent population. In contrast, less than 10% of Canadian dads—for a total of 63,000 men—are staying at home to give their children the dads they deserve (see, again, Shifflett, Peck, Scheller);

12.4/124) a stated preference for the phrase "stay at home dads" as opposed to "stay at home fathers," as the stiffness of the term "father" seems to belie the cargo short, as well as the cargo pant, and also the sheer volume of Lunchables and Honest Kids Organic Strawberry Lemonade juice pouches doled out (at least historically), these latter not distributed by "father" but by "dad," even if the occupation isn't exactly of their own choosing;

12.5/125) the statistic that 80% of those who are SAHD would work full-time outside the home, if they could. Does this make them "bad" parents? To propose an answer to this question, the rejection here of yet *another* Bayesian Network Decision Graph and the adoption, instead, of the sturdy pie chart, with Mom's response—as regards disposition to parenthood—in red and Dad's response in orange, thus avoiding the re-inscription of the overtly sexist attribution of pink and blue.

According to the poll conducted by Parker and Livingston:

% claiming that parenting is
extremely important to their identity:
        Dads—57%
        Moms—58%

% claiming that parenting is *rewarding* all the time:
        Dads—54%
        Moms—52%

% claiming that parenting is *enjoyable* all the time:

    Dads—46%

    Moms—41%

12.6/126) the inclusion of the interesting fact that North Dakota's downstairs neighbor, South Dakota, has the greatest number of SAHDs in the entire country, coming in at 39% (North Dakota claims 13%). What accounts for this regional concentration is probably fascinating and deeply complicated, but it remains at present unknowable. In other words, while reasons for regional concentrations for the SAHD remain oblique, and attitudes towards offspring appear gender-neutral, the foundational conditions of the SAHD phenomena remain, like the fact that 39% of dads in South Dakota are SAHD, perplexing;

13.1/127) an admission that there's currently a risk of having run a little afield of the foundational premises contained in the initial argument (see "Preface"), which is that America's relationship with Canada requires serious re-examination. As has been elsewhere documented, the problem here is two-fold: 1) Canada is becoming increasingly predatory, selfish and manipulative, and 2) the United States—either from incapacity or denial—is not paying attention to this emergent reality (see: "Attention Economy");

13.2/128) a call for bipartisan cooperation. Our fidelity to public engagement should be "like a drake to the duck, a loyalty like a dog's" (Emerson), by which is presumably meant the domestic dog, the "family dog," who, as a testament to the rewards of its devotion, represents a majority stake in the (USD) $103.6 billion per year spent in the pet industry as a whole;

13.3/129) a brief aside to a more or less related subject, an argument that the recently proposed Ralston processing plant should be located in Freyman, North Dakota, as opposed to the outskirts of Estavan, Saskatchewan, for both historical reasons (i.e., after Swiss-based Nestle, motivated by the popularity of their Friskies brand, acquired the St. Louis based company—its livestock feed business, Purina

Mills, having already been sold to British Petroleum, aka BP—the European parent company parlayed their formerly quintessentially American acquisition onto the global market) as well as regulatory reasons (i.e., whereas US pet food quality and production is overseen by the FDA, the Canadian government's view of pet food production is distinctly *laissez faire*, speaking of loyalty, fidelity and dogs);

[Insert, plate 2: black and white image of a black dog with wistful white markings—possibly the image taken directly off the aforementioned "lost" poster—looking curiously at its photographer? Should it be identified via caption as Portuguese Water Dog, as the vet intimated that it just might be (however improbably), a real needle in the haystack out here in the hinterlands, breed-wise, a real, as they say, *find*? Or is this just an example of what Jorgensen and Kettle term "value bloat," the fetishizing of the acquired purchase after the fact so that its intrinsic value is irrationally inflated?]

13.4/130) an argument that the whole of the Canadian regulatory apparatus is, despite its outward appearance as a liberal nation (witness the jaunty skip of its Prime Minister to the border for the purpose of conveying donuts and Lipton Tea to illegal immigrants before mandated social distancing and closing of the borders) is, as their pet food regulatory problem indicates, singularly self-serving in its leanings. For example, Canada is among the very few countries predicted to actually *benefit* from a tempering climate:

shipping lanes, now unnavigable because of sea ice, will open to nautical traffic, natural gas deposits near the North Pole will be accessible, its population, 90% of which is currently huddled for warmth along its southern border with the US, will be able to migrate into the expansive and suddenly habitable lands of the north;

13.5/131) statistical evidence that Canada's pollution emissions rank 15th out of the top 17 countries with regard to the production of greenhouse gasses, a growth of 17 percent in the twenty years between 1990 and 2010, and getting worse. These increases are a result of a growth in exports of petroleum, natural gas and forest products, all undeniably conclusive evidence that it's enabling, entrenching and, indeed, promoting habits amenable to a warming planet;

13.5/132) a restatement of the logical inference here that the same processes that are making Canada warmer are the same processes that will soon make the south and southwestern regions of the United States so hot as to be ultimately uninhabitable;

13.6/133) a re-statement, also, of inevitabilities. Roughly half of the US population will participate in a south to north migration, thus competing for the limited space on its northern border, approximately 150 million feverish faces pressed against an as-yet invisible wall. This will indicate the beginning of the "hard reckoning" (Morris), justice by meat cleaver and zombie tribunals, meaning mob rule;

13.7/134) a vision of Americans in Ford F150s chased by the Canadian Mounted Police as they speed northward, reading maps in the dark by visor-light, speeding toward the areas under alert for winter white-outs, where, any snowplow driver will tell you, is a refuge, a kind of blind, a space of total calm and centeredness, inasmuch as the white-out forces the totalizing necessity for everything to stop, that one can't move forward—neither pursuer or pursued—creating the absolute erasure of the ambition to proceed. The stopping a complete scrubbing from one's self of all *functional* identity, arrested in a single increment of space and time. Until, suddenly, a little grey emerges, then spidery outlines of tree limbs again, then the trees themselves, and then the light on a lamppost, until the entire world comes into relief once more, and one's forced again to move within it;

13.8/135) a proposition that if being chased like a common criminal isn't bad enough, take Warren's quote that "One of Canada's main goals in this renegotiation [of the North American Free Trade Agreement] is to get the United States to treat our workers better. Canada doesn't want its workers competing with poorly-treated laborers—including workers in the United States." In this way Canada can be seen as possibly conditioning a poachable workforce from within the United States itself—that is, in expectation of the northern migration—which Canada perhaps sees as a host (the continental US) for some sort of economic virus, or some kind of covert economic policy incubator;

13.9/136) a suggestion that perhaps the current administration's placement of recent tariffs on Canadian products (i.e., milk, pine, etc.) were rationalized on the basis that Canada is viewed as a "national security threat." And Prime Minister Justin Trudeau's response? "Canadians, we're polite, we're reasonable, but we also will not be pushed around." A pause here to note the striking contrast in that response between Canada's posture—a laid-back, politically liberal, economically quasi-socialist, perpetually polite and reasonable pot smoker—and its words: combative, hostile, threatening. Clearly, to effectively deal with Canada one must contend with the sum totality of its contradictions;

14.1/137) a turn to Asher Horowitz's book *Economies of Violence* in order to further stress the importance of paying attention to the fraught and sometimes dangerous ways Canada's economy engages with the US economy;

14.2/138) discussion of Horowitz's argument that violence itself is a necessary byproduct of one's intrinsic need to increase one's volume, to add to one's "wealth load." Recall here the processes that manifested themselves in such events as the brawl between NHL fans. Horowitz resuscitates the economic principles put forth by Niccolo Machiavelli to make sense of such violent acts, what he (Horowitz) views as entirely unavoidable altercations. And how he does so in a very specific sense and, perhaps, for dubious, if not downright sinister, motives, which will be gotten into in a moment;

14.3/139) a summary of Horowitz's analysis, which implicitly aligns Machiavelli with Detroit Red Wing fans, while the "ancients," specifically Aristotle and Socrates, can be seen to be aligned with Toronto Maple Leaf fans. In other words, Horowitz undoubtedly pits the Aristotelian notion of the "good life" against the Machiavellian notion of "mere life." So there's Socrates, who famously said that "the unexamined life is not worth living," and Machiavelli, who, Horowitz writes, "always sees the possibilities for argument about what the good life is; but everyone can agree that life itself is a good—so life becomes *the* good [emphasis added]." In this way, life itself becomes commoditized before the reader's very eyes;

14.4/140) a qualitative aside here to describe Horowitz's summation of Machiavelli's notion of economics in general as being as stripped of pretense and romantic sentiment as his source material;

14.5/141) Horowitz's assertion that, for Machiavelli, and therefore, by proxy, Red Wingers, "it is not simply the case that the end justifies the means. The only possible end (a stable order of selfishness checking each other) dictates means where both the purely good act and the purely evil act are both superfluous." That is, Horowitz is promoting the very threadbare and classic idea of "economy" as defined as the most effective results born from the most minimal investment. Put another way: "If we (Americans) catch you (Canadians) stealing from us, we'll bash your friggin' faces in";

14.6/142) a reminder about the income distribution graph *viz-a-viz* Canada v. USA discussed earlier: is there any more effective result born from a more minimally based investment than that of brute violence? Unequivocally, and, unfortunately, no. This is not condoning, but simply rationalizing the behavior. Machiavelli's economics, and Horowitz's, too, by deploying him, merely describes a "struggle among a tightly crowded group of actors, each of whom can only benefit from another's loss";

14.7/143) as promised, Horowitz's motivation for suggesting the line of reasoning summarized and why it is suspect. Forced to be limited to just one, there's the fact that, if economic theory teaches us anything, it's that there's no free space outside of self-interest: Horowitz is a member of the faculty at York University. Where, exactly, is York University located? One perhaps shouldn't be surprised to learn that it's located in Toronto, Canada, and that one could therefore be forgiven for speculating about his nationalistic biases, or what NHL team he's undoubtedly inclined to support;

14.8/144) a statement of the problem that such nationalistic prejudices espoused by Horowitz hinder the possibility to introduce the shape of a more optimistic argument, namely that the United States and Canada could possibly deepen their economic and cultural relationship in a respectful and reciprocal manner, because as economics attempts to reveal the processes that contribute to "how people's lives come to be what they are" (Dasgupta), these processes accrete over time, however slowly;

14.9/145) another reminder for a detailed examination of the complex motivating behavior(s) of the "traitorous army" (Lemon) of Trump-supporting "American heroes" (Hannity) as they demonstrated their fury at, and inside, the US Capital Building;

14.10/146) a more general likening of problems and their remedies to continental drift, as too often they're allowed to continue to go unnoticed and unannounced until, ultimately, an unbridgeable chasm grows between them (a thought, in other words, and its accompanying action are so far removed from each other that the subject's actions appear incomprehensible, if not a bit worrying, from without), as in the case of a child crying: no matter the frequency, one doesn't pause to deliberate *ad infinitum* the source of the child's consternation, but instead one stops whatever one's doing and picks that crying child up (Sears);

15.1/147) a return to the toll the transportation of American and, especially, Canadian energy extraction infrastructure is—or used to have, before the pandemic—exacting on our small, borderland communities;

15.2/148) an example of said toll of transportation found in the discovery that the doctor's family dog, Velcro, didn't simply escape from their garage, as had been previously reported, but sources close to the family have revised that account, detailing how in fact the father was seen taking the dog for a walk, that the dog, who was not harnessed (as is recommended), reared back at the abrupt chortle of a downshift-breaking semi, slipped its collar and, against all expected instincts to the contrary, ran headlong onto Main and was run over. Significantly, the offending truck's registration: Canadian;

15.3/149) a clear message to be surmised by the context of the dog's death. The truck did slam on the breaks, but, as noted earlier, because the street has been reduced to so much gravel, it simply skidded on the pulverized road;

15.4/150) a summarized history of near-misses and similar scares involving people and industrial traffic, so much so that the Freyman Municipal Board was forced to commission a study on what's termed "traffic calming" measures, including the deployment of "road diets," bumps, roundabouts, speed cameras and reflectors, all of them, in their totality, a metaphor for the economic and sociological imperative to simply get everyone to slow down and concentrate on the task at hand, to safely get from point A to. . .point B, a mandate stressed as so critical that a five panel Trellis Bar Graph—with positive symbol (bottom right) and negative symbol (bottom left), both in battleship grey background to allow submarine yellow foreground—announcing results of the deliberations, beginning with:

1)   The road diet, or the constriction of the width of Main Street to reduce speed
Pro: calms traffic
Psychological effect: constricted space equals slowing down
Con: no room for emergency responder vehicles (sheriff, volunteer fire department) to navigate road during an emergency
2)   Speed bumps
Pro: cheap
Psychological effect: anxiety
Con: there goes the suspension
3)   Roundabouts
Pro: none
Psychological effect: absolute disorientation
Con: makes people feel insane (unless European or Canadian, as in Montreal, or, unfortunately, from Washington D.C. [insert plate 3: aerial photo of DuPont Circle])

4)   Speed cameras

Pro: automated

Psychological effect: paranoia

Con: authoritarian

5)   Reflectors, or those little blinking signs that tell one how fast one is going

Pro: eminently portable

Psychological effect: fear, then guilt, then relief—that is, if not caught speeding

Con: emotionally addicting;

15.5/151) the proposal of another strategy altogether being advocated by at least one member of the Freyman municipal board: why, the townsfolk in attendance are asked, do we have such a low opinion of ourselves? Why should we be constantly passed over? Aren't we even worth it? In other words, why can't we be, if not *the*, at least *a* destination?;

15.6/152) a PowerPoint presentation, titled THE COCONUT COVE in multi-colored Times New Roman letters, followed by several color slides of an architectural rendering of an indoor water park resort. One hundred-twenty "suites," an enormous terrarium filled with plants and "aqua-drops," an Old Tyme Ice cream Shoppe, speed and freefall slides, Old Tyme Pizza Parlor, water-dump buckets for the little ones, the Coconut Cove Bar and Grille for the adults;

15.7/153) the following exchange lifted from the transcription of the Freyman Municipal Board minutes—

Citizen 1: "What about a lazy river? You got your inner tube. You got your cup holder on it, maybe. Maybe it [the lazy river] could go through the inside where all the slides are then outside, around the property."
Citizen 2: "That's a good idea, if we were somewhere else. Like a tropical island. Or down in Missouri, even";

15.8/154) an, perhaps incidental, observation that these two citizens seem to forget that they are only the "economic subjects they're speaking" (Krieser), and what they're speaking is a kind of impossible hope, or hope for the impossible. There seems to be a difference here, although perhaps one could be forgiven for being momentarily stretched beyond one's capacity to locate what that difference is, exactly;

15.9/155) a *nota bene*, to be "folded in" somehow by way of the March, 2014, news report in *The Local Shopper* indicating that Freyman once had an illegal dump of radioactive mining waste on the edge of town. An abandoned gas station was found to contain hundreds of filter socks, which are used to capture the solids in flowback water during hydraulic fracturing, and which trap naturally-occurring radioactive debris. Geronimo Joe Jones himself representing the views of the entire Freyman Chapter of the North Dakota's Economic Coalition, quoted as saying "It's not exactly the first thing you want folks to think about when they think about your hometown, radioactive waste." Fortunately, this was some time ago, at least enough time for most of those residing outside of Freyman to forget;

15.10/156) the dog, to complete this chapter full circle, reportedly buried under a maple in the back yard. After the body was interred, not without a great deal of effort (lots of roots, apparently), the father brought his daughter back to the freshly turned soil and explained, in sum, how Velcro's body would begin decomposing, and how the roots of the tree would therefore be nourished by Velcro, how Velcro, in sum, would become part of the living tree, so that Velcro really, truly could be seen as living on in the tree, a kind of rebirth, and that the tree too would one day fall, and the earth would be nourished by its decomposition, that dirt itself is nothing but dead things coming alive, and so on and so forth, simultaneously a kind of micro- and macro-economic introduction to the ontological problem buried before them, including frayed leash and little collar;

15.11/157) the daughter's response to the material contained in 15.10 above: "Huh." And then the recorder. *Always* the recorder. Will she ever stop? Does she want to be grounded, like really, no fool's grounded, like no friends, no nothing, just for five minutes of silence, after being stuck in the house together, basically alone, for all these many months? "Look around, dad," she might say, "I mean, Jesus, dad, what does that even friggin' *mean*?";

15.12/158) proof that the daughter is indeed no one's fool. As incomprehensible as she sometimes is to her father—a kind of teenage performance of apathy—the music generated from her recorder, coming out from within her, proves how she's in possession of such an intensely rich, bewilderingly complex inner-life that is inaccessible to him. *Much more complex*, despite the awful constraints, the comically narrow range of the instrument itself, its desired, *believed* effect by the musician herself, those effects being, in reality, impossible. Such limited choices!;

15.13/159) a detailed list of the paucity of resources—culturally, musically, instrumentally—currently available. Back in the fourth grade when first selecting her instrument, a choice between the recorder and tambourine. And while her father is by no means an expert on music, not at all, in terms of both tone and ability to convey the so-called "more refined marketplace of human emotion" (Benjamin), both the recorder and tambourine always struck him, as he conveyed to his wife back then, the retail equivalent of a Wal-Mart, just one step up from a homemade banjo whose acoustic box is a plastic Cool Whip container, a neck made by a ruler, rubber bands for strings;

Volume II:
Getting Back on Track

CHPT 16:
A SURVEY OF OUR EMOTIONAL INTERCONNECTEDNESS

16.1/160) a turning away now from some of the material costs based on our proximity to Canada and its ambitions to some of the psychological costs of that proximity;

16.2/161) deployment of the insights produced by numerous behavioral economists (collected under the working title *Bordering on the Crazy*) in order to survey the argument that living on the US/Canadian border is to inhabit a register on the bipolar spectrum, where Canadians are associated with the manically cheerful, maddeningly optimistic highs, and Americans are associated with the depressive lows, even as the question proper isn't whether or not they're (both Americans and Canadians) manic or depressed, but how aware they are that they're on the spectrum together in the first place;

16.3/162) the statistic that the need for mental healthcare workers will require an increase of at least 1000% after the pandemic, with a 65% increase in telehealth alone (Wan), and at least twice that amount will be required in Indigenous communities, which are "already woefully underserved" (Burkman);

16.4/163) modern psychiatry's determination that the

foundational malady for both mania and depression is *a* depression, because each individual, Canadian and American alike, has, at the center of their national and individual characters, a black hole, around which their selves—their many selves in innumerable iterations of what is called the "self"—are camped along its (black holes') rim, so that naming the black hole a "depression" is using language wrongly, an understandable paradox (Hawking), given that the black hole is ultimately unnamable, is, by definition, the place where meaning breaks down, so that while "black hole," too, is a metaphor, "depression" is a much more inexact metaphor, inasmuch as depression names the psychological weather—a foul weather front, a bad mood, the ebb and flow of meteorological energies, a psychologically attuned barometric pressure—and the thing-in-itself, the black hole, describes that center where no light escapes, is a complete no-thing, pure anti-matter where even the stuff inside, presumably the good stuff, the hope represented by the names of American/Canadian children, for instance, is vacated because nothing matters here;

16.5/164) a proposal of the possibility that the source of the malady described above is possibly—*diagnostically*—boredom. An economy of boredom? 2:30 on a Wednesday afternoon last summer, 92 degrees ambient temperature, 52 percent humidity, a hazy blue sky, the guttural buzz of a lawnmower somewhere in the faraway distance, the buzz-saw ebb and flow of cicadas, the onslaught quietly raging on at the clinic. Everything's done. There's nothing left to do, the universe collapsing into three choices: porn, beer or some super skunky, home-grown sinsemilla;

16.6/165) at the risk of sounding repetitive, a reclaiming that both Canadians and Americans have a feature that, as inescapable as the black holes existing at the center of every galaxy in the universe, likewise black holes are churning at in the center of their own psychologies. So that just as black holes crucially effect the rotation of stars, solar systems, the weather on planets, and everything else that constitutes a galaxy, so too do psychic black holes crucially effect a personality in relationship to it, resulting in the fact that US and Canadian citizens are not so much defined by their depression, but, instead, psychologically embody their depression, whether they consider themselves depressed or not. Black holes feeding on the space around them, endlessly feeding, never full. The most primitive and universal expression of competition between consumers;

16.7/166) a cost comparison of .5 milligrams clonazepam and 300 milligrams Wellbutrin US v Canada;

16.8/167) NASA's most recent addition to these relational matters in the form of an object they've named Ultima Thule, a "bilobate" consisting of one smaller and one larger lobe (in other words, a thing resembling a snowman) careening in the Kuiper belt, and thus representing, courtesy of the New Horizon space craft, the most distant object ever photographed;

16.9/168) the shape of the object itself (Ultima Thule) as the source of a great deal of speculation. It's thought that the whole was formed from two independent, discreet, autonomous individuals, which, over the course of four to five billion years in orbit of one another finally came together, a process as unusual as it is suggestive, inasmuch as such processes in the universe usually result in a violent collision, as opposed to a gentle merger;

16.10/169) the conflation of human being with the New Horizon spacecraft. For it to travel four billion miles in ten years, it had to have very little mass, had to be reliable and self-sustaining, and had to be able to keep going on a very limited power source while remaining fully operational. "The constraints under which our little interstellar explorer operates," states Alan Stern, Principal Investigator, "are monumental." A message sent by New Horizon takes a full six hours to travel through the dark vacuum of space before it's received and read somewhere in Houston, Florida, or, possibly, Alabama;

Chpt 17:
An Introduction to the Boredom Economy

17.1/170) a Histogram Bar Chart titled "One Morning Tending to Stuff," with activity referenced at the bottom and duration, in minutes, said activity takes to complete on left margin. Pastel palette;

17.2/171) an admission that the second component of the histogram—that of time spent tending to the stuff—is, by definition, forever ongoing. Sample activities, however, are arrayed as follows:

emptied dishwasher (got to have dishes to hold the food and contain the liquids);

loaded dishwasher (dishes need to be cleaned);

unplugged toaster and harpooned stuck bread from filament bracket (got to have the bread toasted);

snaked a U by Kotex Teen panty liner from guest bathroom toilet (got to have panty liners, as well as a toilet, and the house to put the toilet, teen and panty liners in);

cleaned lint from dryer vent (got to have clothes and the means to wash and dry them);

changed light bulb in utility room (got to have light and utilities and a room to house them, as well as the house to hold it all);

plowed driveway (got to have the means to allow access and egress to the house);

donned surgical mask and fueled vehicle at gas station (got to follow the laws of internal combustion and face covering);

read owner's manual for turning off tire pressure differential dash warning light while fueling vehicle (another vehicle requiring proper tire maintenance);

checked tire pressure (x4) (tires generally requiring air);

put air in two tires (optimal vehicle operation requiring equal amounts of air in all tires; see, also: drive train);

contemplated the abstract notion of slipping clutches (just in case the clutch starts slipping);

plowed three driveways, all "private clients" (got to pay for the gas and put some money away for a rainy day clutch-fund);

donned surgical mask to buy light bulbs and AA batteries at Len's Hardware (last light bulb having been used in the utility room);

monitored morphine drip for five minutes (certain deaths accompanied by agony);

replaced batteries in remote control (the remote control not working last night interfering with the abstract notion of "entertainment" in the room most commonly lived in inside the house);

Windexed dog snot from the lower quadrant of the foyer windows (preemptive erasure of animal stain);

salted sidewalk and driveway (ensuring safer egress and entrance to the house);

rethreaded torsion screw on adjustable music stand (can't be expected to memorize all the notes on all the music pages in all the music books), momentarily considering whether or not to throw the stand away, as well as all the books, and all the other stuff as well;

per favor, because reminded a million times already over the course of numerous phone calls, folded sweaters "nicely" on the top closet shelf in the "master bedroom" (got to keep all the stuff organized and in order);

hiding recorder between nicely folded sweaters (got to spare the aspiring musician future ridicule and the devastating revelation that what the aspiring musician held so dear was so fundamentally absurd, finally, even if attainable at some so-called level of "mastery." Could it even be said *worthless*?);

flushing handle unaccountably disengaged, removed toilet tank cover and manually engaged the flushing mechanism, noting that it needs to be attended to tomorrow;

18.1/172) an introduction to the notion that Canada experiences a "crises of personality," has a muddled, nearly schizophrenic disposition similar to an Australian's, who on the one hand is by temperament an isolationist, but on the other is almost pathologically responsive when some international tragedy or other plays out in front of their wet, blue eyes;

18.2/173) the observation that international tragedy seems to elicit in them (Canadians) a response as generously empathetic as it is naïve, as evident in the illustrative case of Canada's response to the CBN's footage captured immediately after the earthquake in the Haitian capital Port-au-Prince (circa 2010);

18.3/174) a referencing of those scenes depicting the looting of a supermarket there (Port-au-Prince), outside of which a reporter stands next to the supermarket's owner, who has been explaining in broken, sometimes translated English how he's worked his whole life at the supermarket, that the supermarket was started by his father, handed down to his son—here the current owner swats tears visibly rolling down his cheeks—while the mob behind him, reportedly in the hundreds, pours in and out of the shattered storefront with small bales of what are clearly identifiable as Pampers, cellophane sleeved loaves of Wonder Bread, cases of canned goods, gallons of milk, boxes of snack cakes or crackers stacked to their chins like library books;

18.4/175) successive images of the pillaging of staples that results in the Haitian supermarket owner to be emotionally overcome, causing the reporter to place a hand on his heaving shoulder, patting it, telling him (the owner) how sorry he (the reporter) is, when from the right of the screen a white Ford Explorer arrives, delivering four uniformed Haitian security officers, forcing the crowd to scatter, dropping their ill-gotten booty as they alight;

18.5/176) a reminder: "failed coup" (Cuomo) carried out by "violent Antifa infiltrators" among Trump supports at US Capital. An analysis of the potent symbol of protestor defecating and urinating in its (the US Capital Building's) hallways;

18.6/177) the re-establishment of the rule of law and order in Port-au-Prince. A series of scenes depicting the devastating aftermath of the earthquake, which causes all of Canada to stay their knives mid-way through a raspberry brie, making them put down their marginally well-hopped IPA on the counter in order to marshal a response that eventually results in a Hercules-class Canadian Air Force cargo transport loaded with diapers, formula and unisex one-sies to circle the already overwhelmed Port-au-Prince airport in seemingly endless loops until it's eventually rerouted to Miami International Airport, much to Canada's visible disgust, frustration and anguish;

CHPT 19:
SOME PROPHETIC, ECONOMICAL POETRY FROM THE 17TH CENTURY ENGLISH POET WILLIAM BLAKE

19.1/178) speculation on the following lines, which could possibly even work as an epigraph to this project:

> On the Canadian wilds I fold; feeble my spirit folds,
> . . . .
> It joy'd [.];

19.2/179) an assertion that in his "Preludium" to *America: A Prophecy* (from which the lines are taken), William Blake (1757-1827)—English illustrator, printmaker, essayist, poet (Wikipedia)—offers an early examination of the historically contentious relationships on the North American continent, ascribing Mexico, NAFTA's dusty doormat to the south, with an eagle, and a serpent with Canada;

19.3/180) Canada-as-snake transmogrifying a little later into Canada as "hairy shouldered...terrible boy" breathing "pestilence" on the "banquet" that America—"Invulnerable though naked, save where the clouds roll round her loins"—offers "it," revealing, arguably, the poet's proclivity for passionate feeling over diplomacy, when of course diplomacy is what's required in these "complex" (Clinton) international matters;

19.4/181) Blake's notion that the "God that dwells over Canada" is the "image of God who dwells. . .in regions of dark death." His own reaction to this bleak geography: it's "drinking my soul away." It's as if he'd just prophesized the cause of his own demise. The apparently famous melancholic dies at age 69 of liver disease in Westminster, London, fat-ravaged heart of that corrupt and corrupting empire—notwithstanding that this place, too, is something of a hole, though of a much more rural example;

19.5/182) the raising of what might be considered contract issues: how, for example, as is the case in any relationship, hostile rhetoric doesn't advance a way forward, but instead detracts from recognizing the underlying benefits of, perhaps, a more reciprocal view of our human and natural resources;

19.6/183) a reconsideration of how to move away from the introductory remarks ("A Preface," "A Note on Method") to more strategic concerns inherent in the plan itself, and the discovery of how any claim of authority in this era of "fake news" (Bannon) potentially invokes an immediate suspicion, which might make bringing the completed work to market an especially tricky business;

19.7/184) a few thoughts on how market forces themselves need to be contended with. The term "market," of course, signifying constituent consumers, those who would be presumably consuming this content after the labor was spent producing it, a rather familiar transaction enacted in the formerly white (and formerly empty) field, whereupon, like blacktop under a blanket of snow, this sort of transaction typically takes place;

19.8/185) a few more thoughts on the general shape of the contract, already somewhat strained and perhaps prohibitively overly-constructed. A comparisons of the potential publication date of the completed work to the date of its being consumed. Should this be measured in months, years, decades? In the interim, has the European Union held? Are these United States still united? In other words, rather than going into the Blake poem, perhaps instead further consideration on the intervening span of time that might determine meaning and reception (e.g., see, again, the notion of "contract");

19.9/186) the fact that on the day this plan was started, anyone present needed to self-regulate and engage in some silent activity, because the bifocaled eyeglasses were present, the wine was in the water glass, the work was being presently produced, and even our most beloved musical instruments, as Paganini, or somebody like him, famously put it, yes, even our most beloved instruments sometimes needed to be put away for awhile in their cases;

Chpt 20:
Some More People Just Passing Through

20.1/187) a group of strangers, who suddenly arrived the autumn before the pandemic and first appeared, from a distance, as discreet individuals onto the Piggy Wiggly parking lot, and who were now beginning to cohere into the appearance of family unit—presumably a mother, father, child—moving steadily forward across the hot asphalt field, as if nothing more than an impending announcement of more certain information. A harbinger of things to come;

20.2/188) the thought that this must have been what the townspeople experienced in the days of the pony-express, when one could *see* the flow of information, experience it, at the cantering speed of a tired pony's gait. Meaning: a message arriving via human locomotion, a kind of persistent amble weighted by luggage, and further hobbled by its slowest member, a young boy, who was being fairly dragged along by the presumed mother, herself perhaps sensing the impatience of their audience, comprised at this moment of three cashiers and an Assistant Manager from the grocery store, several on-looking customers, a teenager hunched over her phone, and a man on his John Deere, who seemed to have inadvertently mowed his way onto the scene;

20.3/189) the not entirely unexpected nature of the family's arrival. Yesterday, or today or tomorrow, the leadership of Freyman warned—not a matter of *if*, but *when*, so the town was not completely caught off guard. Transcripts of official proceeding published in *The Shopper*, official and unofficial reports directly communicated by the Freyman municipal government to the public, general rumor, as well as the periodic apprisels of developments as warranted. Trailways, for example, opening up a new route to accommodate them (the strangers), announcing that they would begin delivering passengers to the BP off exit 217, midway between Bristol and Green Grass, a point on the map a half-mile south of Freyman. The cashier at the gas station instructed to hand out business cards with a local car service number, if the travelers desired to be picked up, which was evidently not the case with the family walking toward the informal and hastily assembled welcoming committee;

20.4/190) the man's (presumably the woman's husband, the boy's father) thin and short stature, a face suggesting middle-age, until those structures around the eyes were surveyed up close, which, as is the clique, appear much older, much more worn, almost damaged-looking by a persistently bad weather. His greying hair cut very short, his nose long and thin;

20.5/191) likewise recalled, an enormous roller-duffle dragged behind the man, whose clothes were a mix-match of brands and period styles, so that he looked like a walking advertisement for economic globalization, or, perhaps more fairly, someone who had moved across enormous parts of the globe, and, like a passport collecting visas, wore the mark of his travels on his body: the cuffs and pleats of his gabardine trousers suggesting Herrods, that iconic British department store, circa 1968, which were nevertheless too roomy for his diminutive frame, so that the waist of his pants were hitched up high above his anatomical waist with a thin belt;

20.6/192) an image of the top button of the man's collarless dress shirt cinched, the sleeves rolled up past his elbows. Did the style of the shirt hail from the Middle-East, Mexico or the Cowboy's Crossing and Emporium in Bismarck?;

20.7/193) a pair of dusty, white, high top sneakers sporting the distinct, bi-color F of the Italian Fila brand;

20.8/194) the woman (presumably the man's wife, the boy's mother) draped in a light pink robe, which reached, hood-like, over her head and fell to mid-calf, themselves (her calves) covered to the ankles by black leggings. On her feet, rubber flip-flops, the kind and quality that can be purchased at Wal-Mart for ninety-nine cents;

20.9/195) the boy holding onto the woman's hand. His other held an aluminum lunchbox emblazoned with the menacing-looking robot Megatron, familiar enough to those old enough to remember the *Transformer* cartoons. The family and their welcome party all proceeded to smile, nod, shake hands, make pronouncements that were undoubtedly incomprehensible to at least half the parties present at any given moment, including the fact that a $20 gift certificate (where did that come from?) had been donated to the family by the grocery store behind them;

20.10/196) the man holding out his arms, and how he then began making a gesture like he's milking a cow. Accompanying this milking motion, the singularly understandable word "Canada";

20.11/197) an interval of approximately twenty seconds into this performance, when one of the cashiers finally discerned that the gesture signified one steering a steering wheel, and that the man was inquiring into the car service;

20.12/198) another durational space of approximately ten minutes, at the end of which the family climbed into the back of a rusted red Chevy Trailblazer, waving their hands out the window, heading the one and a half miles north to the US-Canadian border, leaving those left behind to wonder, among numerous other things, what, exactly, it meant that they didn't redeem the gift certificate;

20.13/199) a transition to a cobalt blue Singer Graph displaying the five most prominent communities of immigrants to Canada last year:

Syria—33,266
USA—6,664
Eritrea—3,934
Iraq—1,650
Congo—1,644 ;

CHPT 21:
HOMETOWN CURRENCY

21.1/200) the notion of *town* in general taken up;

21.2/201) a theory of how, initially settled on hope, any town endeavors to participate in a matrix built upon a complex set of both interdependent relations and competition with other towns. In other words, whose town is advanced, for example, when the rural dweller says "I'm going to town," when the sweetheart says "take me to town," when the hung-over had their "night on the town"?;

21.3/202) even more germane to this part of the plan, perhaps: what of the town that finds itself unable to see itself relationally, finds itself ignored, a geographical transom to pass through, a drive-by, but never a destination *per se*? An awareness here that this concern was voiced earlier by other voices. But still, what becomes of its initial promise, that first hope? Do these towns, like those who experience popularity when young, find themselves in middle age alone, isolated, maybe grown just a little bitter, yearning for a past they can barely remember, a past entirely devoid of concrete image, but nonetheless felt?;

21.4/203) a memory of the feeling of being a force of attraction, a moment, however long or short, when their (both the town and its people, that is) very presence was a warp in space around which others were pulled into orbit. And now here they are, as if flung out alone into the cold, empty space of the universe, a suddenly small seeming, suddenly insignificant object suspended in dark matter, a somewhere whose being is no longer enough, or, worse, whose being has become intolerable;

21.5/204) a proposal that Freyman (North Dakota, USA) adopt Estevan (Saskatchewan Province, Canada) as its "sister city," a delineation of the intrinsic benefits resulting therefrom, including the lifting of all international tariffs on pharmacological products and the easing of international travel restrictions, shared water resources, liberalized exchange of "bucks" to "loonies," and vice-versa, without having to pay the outrageous brokerage fees to an intermediary for the privilege of said currency exchanging hands, so that a more generally broad exchange of goods and services between the two countries might be established, an absolute "duty-free" zone between Freyman and Estevan that might facilitate a form of "barter" economy, where such behind-the-counter products sold only by prescription in the US—trans-spectrum antibiotics, dermatology-grade localized melanoma lightening cream, high-potency anti-inflammatories targeting herniated disks, migraine headaches and the like—and which are available much more cheaply over-the-counter in Canada might be "swapped" for deeply discounted American goods: rhinoplasty, lung aspirations, CAT scans;

21.6/205) a notion of currency—or, more specifically, the possibility of a micro-currency—floated in an effort to elaborate upon a cooperative, albeit regional, US/Canadian model, one based largely on the German experience, whose twenty-four (and counting) local micro-currencies (the Kingower, the Havelbluete) promote regional investment by "building in" a 2% depreciation rate if the currency is not used within a specific amount of time, said 2% "penalty" being donated to local nonprofits (school lunch programs, new pavement);

21.7/206) the possibility that Germany is left out of this discussion altogether, and instead US local currencies are exclusively considered. Witness the Berkshares (Berkshire County, MA) and Ithaca Hours (Ithaca, NY). Or even Bitcoin, the cryptocurrency used in digital payment transactions, the 21st century's symbol of pure faith;

[insert, plate 4: artist rendering of the "Freedom Exchange," described as a "living monument" to US/Canadian relations in the form of a two mile length of red cobble stone (connoting strength, solidity, history, shared blood) road between Freyman and Estevan, a tastefully executed "mall" (in the best sense of its commercial and commemorative aspects) supporting international enterprises laid out earlier, terminating on the one end at the campus of a proposed Minot Community College/Freyman Annex, and, at the other end, the (already existing) Academy of Learning Computer and Business Career College, in Estevan, signifying the importance of education to prosperity, all of it lined with ginkgo saplings, planted in a summer-long ceremony by an equal number of mothers and their daughters—further extrapolated to include an equal number of US and Canadian citizens— to suggest the process by which knowledge is "passed down," to borrow a phrase from the local Indigenous Peoples, through the generations, the continuum of "birthing" knowledge into subsequent generations through the wisdom and experience of both countries' forebears, creating, as these most ancient trees eventually grow skyward, a dappled shade made more glorious and expansive year by year by ever-loving year...]

22.1/207) a further discussion of Bitcoin as a transnational currency, which itself provides an opportunity to introduce the concepts of "weighted" and "weightless" economies. The weighted economy names the material economy, the production of goods and their component parts: lead, for example, and automobiles, paper currency and coinage divorced from symbolism, cement, diamonds, human bodies, kiwis, tungsten, Wheaties, wood, etc. The weightless economy, by contrast, names those seemingly ephemeral and invisible processes upon which the material economy is entirely dependent: personhood, trust, the literalization of symbolism (as in currency itself), beauty, etc.;

22.2/208) a focus on those elisions wherein the material transitions into the weightless, a *chrysopea* (i.e., "transmutation") familiar to alchemists. One thinks here of the unseemly sites on the dark web where anyone so inclined (and monied in a sufficient amount of Bitcoinage) can purchase an entire identity. This is a weightless economy gaining weight. The process begins with the foundational question, "who do you want to be?" A fundamental question often answered with more fantasy than aspiration: to be a younger woman, say, in your early thirties (the obvious constraint here being passability). And what about nationality? "American" is evidently the most sought-after, and consequently the most costly;

22.3/209) a class status here purchased by a series of pull-down menus that offer various bank, tax and credit fraud schemes, primarily built upon others' true identities, all of which remain an artifact of the weightless economy. It's only when the impersonator begins acquiring material evidence of the identity—social security card, credit cards, birth certificate, passport, driver's license—that the identity becomes sufficiently weighted to operate in the primary market, what many economists refer to as the "real world" (Paulson, Clapper, Schniderman, et al.);

22.4/210) the inclusion of the concept of the "repulsion economy" as a principle way to mitigate such calamities as identity theft. A consideration of the recent moves made by Equifax in an attempt to minimize the appalling statistic that roughly half of adult Americans had their social security, credit card, driver's license numbers and home addresses hacked from their data system, effectively creating the possibility that half of adult Americans might have their identity stolen in perpetuity. By withholding this information from consumers for three full months, then releasing it just as hurricane Irma was bearing down on the Florida peninsula, Equifax sprung their terrible news onto an American public already over-satiated with bad news, thereby preemptively repulsing it before it might otherwise begin to digest the information;

22.5/211) a description of the way businesses, politicians and whole countries frequently engage in repulsive economic warfare, as do "regular people." One thinks here of a garbage can. If one wanted to deter others from looking into the garbage can, along with the "regular" garbage, one might also strategically include a quantity of dog feces, for example (the massive amount of which is gathered daily in America's backyards), as well as the occasional dead rodent (a squirrel killed by the aforementioned dog, for instance, or a mouse caught in a glue trap in the basement, or a robin that broke its neck crashing into the window), all of which, after a very brief period of time, would contribute to such an affront to the senses that any sensitive personal information daily disposed of would, through repulsion, be protected, be these credit card, retirement or bank statements, a quantity of empty beer and/or wine bottles, or sensitive medical information, of course;

1

23.1/212) before the pandemic and the Turtle Mountain Reservation outbreak, a sidling up, Malinowski-style, to a Canadian specimen encountered at the Speak Easy Bar, who is at first hidden in a distraction, a problem, commonly known as "Frankel's Promise," which states that every major contemporary *issue* is fundamentally an *economic* problem, one that, Frankel promises, is solvable by an economic *solution*;

23.2/213) the total embodiment of an interruption, it's here that the Canadian fully announces himself by slamming an empty pint glass on the bar, causing his red packet of Du Maurier cigarettes to take an almost imperceptible hop, the short stack of bills (US currency in various denominations) to faintly flutter, a fistful of coins and car keys rattling in recoil after the pop of the glass against the water-ringed oak;

23.3/214) a Canadian, who, so unlike his dying counterpart bathed in the perpetual flickering of the Hallmark Channel, stands tall and healthy;

23.4/215) a Canadian, wearing a Toronto Maple Leaf jersey beneath his unzipped parka, shouting obscenities at the television bolted high on the wall, broadcasting a hockey game;

23.5/216) this entirely unsolicited information, doled out over some twenty minutes: he's a derrickman on one of the Bakken Deposit frakpads some thirty miles due west. He's flopping at the Roughneck Bunkhouse here in town because it's the closest place he could find, that he's not from around here, that he's Canadian, that he's sorry if he's talking too much but he's, like, maybe a little *drunk*, okay, and has taken a little *something* to lighten the mood around here. And with that, he fades for now, like Ebenezer Scrooge's apparition of a possible future;

2

23.6/217) a coywolf. What's a coywolf? To understand, another recollection of Velcro, the dog that was first found out to have escaped from the garage, then his harness, then was run over. His true fate seems at first take to be so unbelievable that it had to be independently verified with some impromptu research. Sources include the Smithsonian on-line, a *National Geographic*, the mammalogist Matthew Gompper and somebody name-dropped into the research simply as a mysterious "Dr. Kay":

Q: so what's a "coywolf?"
A: a coywolf is a hybrid canine. DNA in scat samples reveal its composition typically as 1/4 wolf, 3/5 coyote and 1/10

domestic dog, the latter typically a large breed, such as a German Shepard or Doberman Pinscher;

Q: where do coywolves orginate?

A: the first documented coywolf appeared around 1919 in Ontario, Canada;

Q: what is the difference between an American coyote and a Canadian coywolf?

A: the average Midwestern coyote weighs between 24 and 31 pounds. Canadian coywolves are generally 55 pounds heavier than the average coyote of the Midwestern region of the United States. Coywolves also have a larger jaw, smaller ears and a bushier tale;

Q: are coywolves "fearsome predators?"

A: according to Dr. Kay, coyotes dislike hunting in the forest. Wolves prefer it. Interbreeding has produced an animal skilled at catching prey in the open terrain and densely wooded areas alike. Their cries, a blend of those two ancestors. The first part of a howl resembles the resonant pitch of a wolf's, but this then turns into a higher-pitched, coyote-like yipping;

Q: like what's been heard somewhat more frequently in the northern regions of America, about which many have maybe even wondered aloud? As in, like, what *is* that?

A: reportedly;

Q: what does a coywolf's diet consist of?

A: coywolfs eat rabbits and deer. Carrion, too. And blueberries and raspberries. In fact, blueberries and raspberries can make up half their diet in the late summer months!

Q: do coywolfs eat cats?

A: yes. Coywolfs are opportunistic hunters. They are known to occasionally eat cats;

Q: do coywolfs eat dogs?

A: yes. Smaller dogs, especially. Especially when left unattended;

Q: so professional consensus (eg., dog trainers, vets), not to mention common sense, indicates that smaller dogs should *never* be unattended, yes?

A: well, there's the ideal and then there's lived life. Take your "time out," for example. For the dog, that is. Say it chewed the tongue off a snow boot. Whatever. Younger dog behavior. Your typical naughty dog stuff. What're you supposed to do? Whack him? Hit him with a broom handle?

Q: professional consensus indicates that a dog, young or old, big or small, should *never* be hit. Agreed?

A: so how's he going to learn his lesson, right? Maybe tie him to a post in the backyard for ten minutes. A more passive, non-violent response to correct the underlying problem of footwear destruction. But shows him who's boss just the same, who's the alpha in this little pack;

Q: there's something ominous going on here;

A: that's all it takes for a coywolf. Ten minutes is a long time for a coywolf. In one example, a youngish, smallish black and white dog is found on its side in the slush of red snow, its head planted on the icy ground, jaw down, in an anatomically peculiar angle indicative of a broken neck. The left ear is gnawed off, as is the scalp on that side. His abdomen is an eviscerated pocket of shredded seams. The right hind leg is chewed off at the ankle. Sex organs are missing, as is the rectum;

Q: you get the sense that one had to stand here agape for a long time to register these details;

A: alternatively, roadkill (aka "highway pizza," "flat meats"), both as a distraction but also to provide a broader context, stacked and served up in an infograph, to include 41 million squirrels, 26 million cats, 22 million rats, 19 million opossums, 15 million raccoons, 6 million dogs, and 350,000 deer run down on US roads yearly. Exclusive of birds (approx. 27 million). Exclusive of insects (approx. 32.5 trillion). Some species known to willingly sacrifice themselves to being roadkill;

Q: a momentary allowance of the conceptualization of suicide as smell—a detergent, bright and hollow and clean—suggesting suicide not as a retreat into death, but a return to innocence, which requires an admission of the totalizing corruption of living right before the ego returns one, completely, to blinding fear;

A: the word *baseline* used in a sentence: the baseline average is where human beings are marking their mortality;

Q: a non sequitur. What were Portuguese Water Dogs bred for in the first place?

A: Portuguese Water Dogs were originally bred to deliver messages between ships in the olden days, and also to help detangle fishing lines and nets, and, also, to tow the line. Therefore a particularly mouthy breed;

Q: the dog's function in the family unit seen similarly. The dog charging to and fro among the discreet family members creating a message of unity, coherence, a moving target upon which they can focus their communal attention;

A: or something like that;

Q: the dog often diffusing tensions (i.e., untangling lines of communication) by sheer force of his enormous personality (at once clever, naughty, happy, in a word used by the family itself, "spicy"). Towing the line. An unusual breed, especially in these parts, so says the local veterinary community. And yet, despite the improbability, can't one think themselves just a little lucky every now and then? Thoughts?

A: thoughts that seem to give structure to this sadness. And probably ones best kept to one's self;

CHPT 24:
A Re-formulation

24.1/218) another go at the perplexing problem introduced by the SAHD state of affairs. So let:

1. (אh/:) # ב

Wherein:

א = an infinite cardinality, the number of elements in a set with infinite possibilities; also, an aleph number, ultimately unmappable, so that every space on the map, so to speak, represents the site of a "fresh start"

h = pre-Hilbert space. What's this? It's oblique significance to be thoroughly developed later? [insert, plate 5: tonal image made on an oscilloscope]

/ = divisor

: = inner-product space, a vector space within which is embedded another vector space, possibly a theory of love, the end of the paradoxical singularity represented by א

= connected sum, a homeomorphism in topology, whereby two independently mapable spaces deform, stretch and bend each other into one mapable space while preserving all the topological properties of their initial mappings [insert, plate 6: Morgenstern cartoon illustrating oft-repeated caption that "topologists can't tell their coffee cups from their doughnuts"]

ℶ = beth number, also representing an infinite cardinality, but not necessarily those possessed by ℵ. Not to be confused with a lady named Beth!

2. (ℵh/:) # ℶ → [(ℵh/:) # ℶ + ⨿Xi (∀,∃,∃!)] = ∈

Wherein:
→ = function vector: "from…to"
+ = an addition
⨿ = co-product
X = dependent variable, where (-i) substitutes for infant (+i)
∀ = universal quantification: "for all"
∃ = existential quantification: "there exists"
∃! = uniqueness quantification: "there exists exactly one"
∈ = set membership [insert, plate 7: Levin still-frame from the iconic film *Baby Makes Three*]

3. ∈ᶜ(Tn) ∩ Tn(GDP + H)°

Wherein:
∩ = conditional probability
GDP = gross domestic product
H = housing starts
° = optimal condition: for construction contractors, a US GDP that maintained or surpassed first quarter 2006 levels of 5.4% and housing starts that maintained or surpassed first quarter 2006 levels of 1,789,932 units

4. $\underline{\in C(Tn)} \cap (GDP + H)^\circ = (\aleph h/:) \rightarrow C(Tm,Td,Tn,Tr,Ta,Tp...Tx)$
$\qquad (GDP + H)^-$

Wherein:

$^\circ$ = suboptimal condition: for construction contractors, a US GDP that fell to first quarter 2009 levels of -4.8% and housing starts that fell to first quarter 2009 levels of 513,477 units

C = 2001 Chrysler PT Cruiser convertible (hunter green, khaki rag top) complete with towing package for transporting utility trailer, tools

m = Madison, WI

d = Des Moines, IA

n = Nashville, TN

r = Raleigh, NC

a = Atlanta, GA

p = Pensacola, FL

5. $[(\aleph h/:) \rightarrow C(Tf,Td,Tn,Tr,Ta,Tp...Tx)] - \in = \emptyset$

Wherein:

- = subtraction

$\emptyset$ = empty set

6. $\in [C(Tm \rightarrow Tn - Tm)] = \in C(Tn)$

Wherein:

C = cardinality of the continuum

T = topology (general)

m = topology, specific to Madison, WI

n = topology, specific to Freyman, ND

7. $$\frac{\varnothing}{\beth + \coprod Xi\ (\forall,\exists,\exists!)} = \ \sim \mathbb{P}[\beth + \coprod Xi\ (\forall,\exists,\exists!)]$$

Wherein:

~ = probability distribution

$\mathbb{P}$ = projective space, at the near end of which is something like the formaldehyde stink of pressure-treated decking lumber, and at the far-far end, something like the black surface of the Boundary Dam Reservoir reflecting the phosphorescent glow of Canada, all lit up in yellow electric light in the summer night. There's just so much water on their side;

24.2/219) a note. As is evident, this re-evaluation doesn't formulate an account of the phenomena of SAHD-concentration in the lower Dakota, which is beyond the scope of this study. One could, however, simply apply some common sense here. For if one were prepared to accept the possibility that, in areas where traditional roles prevail a stay-at-home-dad might be shunned by stay-at-home moms' socialization groups, then South Dakota might be viewed as being both more supportive and welcoming of the SAHD population because of the large number who already identify as such;

24.3/220) the conclusion that given its comparatively very low SAHD population, it would necessarily follow that North Dakota is both shunning and isolating, that there's no one to even have a cup of coffee with while the kids do whatever it is they do when they're out there (wherever), when they're not on some infantile play-date anymore, but just "hanging out"....that is, when their allowed to go out at all;

CHPT 25:
RATIONAL ACTORS;

25.1/221) the earlier reference of behavioral economist Amiya Kumar Dasgupta presenting here an opportunity to introduce the concept of rational and irrational actors;

25.2/222) Canada accusing the United States of being irrational, and the United States accusing Canada of acting irrationally. The bickering continues. But there just seems to be more and more of it lately. A wealth load of bickering;

25.3/223) the neoclassical economists' assertion that rational behavior is optimizing behavior (Tufts). Hence the famous rationality axiom that a rational person maximizes their self-interest. However, the choices made in the pursuit of self-interest assume that rational actors have "perfect" information at their disposal, or, at the very least, will collect information (information, that is, that informs the decision making process) until the estimated costs of acquiring more information exceeds the estimated benefits;

25.4/224) a question: how to know when to stop acquiring information to make the optimal choice? What *is* an optimal choice? When is it known? When does one lean in, for example, and endeavor to consummate the first kiss? When to rear back from an embrace? For what reason? What sort of unknowable chain of events will be produced by these decisions?;

121

25.5/225) Herbert Simon's speculation about the impossibility of knowing when all the information that's required for optimal choice-making is acquired. A sort of mental illness. All of this data gathering—rather, trying to divine the cost/benefit ratio of data gathered, for which the psychologist received a Nobel Memorial Prize in economic science in 1978. What's achieved instead, to use the Nobel award winner's word, is a state of "satisfice." Without the ability to know the optimal point of every decision, big and small, one flinches, one cowers, and then one simply seeks the "best" mode to arrive at a satisfying outcome;

25.6/226) more questions: what's "best"? Who decided this? Choice after choice after choice, that's life. Put another way, life: look at the choices that make it;

25.7/227) the supposition that at least one way people try to compensate for the fact that, at some moment, one needs to stop collecting information and choose is through the word "melioration," defined as the ancient striving to do better. Classic examples in this regard include fishermen and potentially unfaithful spouses. A fisherman, only able to keep one fish, will fish the entire day, constantly "trading up" for larger and larger fish, throwing the smaller fish back. In this way, at the end of the day, the fisherman will have the largest fish possible. Likewise trading up is the foundational rationale for the potentially unfaithful spouse. Note that for the fisherman, however, history matters: is this fish bigger than the last fish? for example. For the possibly cheating spouse, it probably doesn't matter at all (e.g., "what, *our* history? *What* history?"). History in fact is often obliterated in the latter case, especially with lithe Canadian boys, totally unconcerned with catching or spreading Covid-19, prowling the local bars like packs of coywolves, or even some handsome, long-haired, infirm local, regardless his infirmity;

26.1/228) having discussed the notion of acting rational, a turn now to the notion of irrational actors;

26.2/229) Richard Lipscombe summoned as especially useful in a discussion of irrationality, especially his commentary on the Union Carbide tragedy that occurred in Bhopal, India, where approximately 5,200 people died as a result of a gas leak in the plant. Acknowledging the human tragedy, which, he confesses, he's powerless to do anything about, he focuses on Union Carbide's share price, which predictably went down. Sellers immediately began to reduce their share price, hoping to lure potential buyers scared off by the spectacle of the tremendous human suffering inflicted upon the Indigenous Indian population;

26.3/230) the sell-off of Union Carbide stock by Union Carbide investors ensuring the financial crises of the very company they owned stock in. This in itself is clear evidence of irrational behavior, but it's also, Lipscombe argues, evidence of the emergence of what he calls the "victim economy," a new economic model promoted by everyone from "the Pope to a dinner host," essentially anyone bemoaning the inequalities and attendant social injustice issues that exist in America (although why a dinner host is implicated here—in other words, just what assumptions are being made about the dinner host—isn't quite clear in his account);

26.4/231) a subsequent summary of Lipscombe's argument that the victim economy will usurp what many economists see as the next emergent economic model, the "sharing economy" (i.e., various ride-share companies and home vacation rental brokerages, which are at present participating in lively sharing communities);

26.5/232) Lipscombe's revelation of the paradox that the sharing economy is a novel approach to an old problem— that is, how to organize assets in order to generate revenue—without offering a "productive reconceptualization" of the problem in the first place. The victim economy, on the other hand, creates communities of consumers based on victimization. Liscombe's penultimate example of this is climate change, in the face of which there is growing pressure from potential global warming victims (including their unborn children! or so he says) for the restructuralization of basic business models not based on "new technology, new products, new services, new ways of doing things" but on how people experience their lives as a part of a victim collective, "be that informed by gender, minority status, wealth (and lack thereof) or politics";

26.6/233) a re-reading of the Canadian J.J. McCullough's article "I'm Canadian, but Trump's got a point about unfair trade" in the *Washington Post* to understand more fully Canada's historic claim of victimization. One needs to appreciate, he writes, "Canada's unique psychological anxiety about being conquered by the United States, and the savvy manner in which Canadian special interests have capitalized on this fear to push protectionist exemptions for themselves in the name of 'sovereignty'";

26.7/234) finally, together with sharing and victimizing, an introduction to the idea of the "economics of proportionality." The sentiment from the Roaring Twenties frames it concisely when the flapper asks this question: "if you awake at 3am, when, then, is the cocktail hour?" Assuming the average American worker rises at 7am, is at work by 9am, and ends the day at 5pm, then it stands to reason that 5pm is time for cocktails. Ergo: 10 hours pass between 7am and 5pm, which puts the cocktail hour for those who rise at 3am at 1pm. Suffice it to say that everything's indeed proportional and relative;

27.1/235) as regards energy production and reciprocal trade, the exceedingly complex, contentious and nuanced subject of competition between Canada and the United States is at last thoroughly examined by way of Locke, Adams, Kant, Rousseau, Hampton, Buchanan, Hobbes, Hume, Narveson, Rawls, Gauthier, et. al.;

27.2/236) as an example on the subject of commerce, Locke: "All the imaginable ways of increasing Money in any Country, are these two: Either to dig it in Mines of our own, or get it from our Neighbours. . .The way of getting from Foreigners, is either by force, borrowing, or trade. And whatever ways besides these, Men may fansie, or propose, for increasing of Money, (except they intend to set up for the Philosophers Stone) would be much the same with a Distracted Man's device that I knew, who, in the beginning of his Distemper first discover'd himself to be out of his Wits, by getting together, and boiling a great number of Groats, with a design, as he said, to make them plim, i.e. grow thicker";

27.3/237) as an example on the subject of trade, Adams: "By the fourth of the rules annexed to the Old Subsidy, the drawback allowed upon the exportation of all wines amounted to a great deal more than half the duties which were, at that time, paid upon their importation; and it seems, at that time, to have been the object of the legislature to give somewhat more than ordinary encouragement to the carrying trade in wine. . .the interest of so large a sum occasioned an expense, which made it unreasonable to expect any profitable carrying trade in this article";

27.4/238) as an example on the inherent role of self-interest and selfishness in commerce and trade, Kant: "Anything is 'Mine' by right, or is rightfully mine, when I am so connected with it, that if any other person should make use of it without my consent, he would do me a lesion or injury. The subjective condition of the use of anything is possession of it. An external thing, however as such could only be mine, if I may assume it to be possible that I can be wronged by the use which another might make of it when it is not actually in my possession";

27.5/239) a quick backward flip here, the landing stuck back onto the Bakken Shale deposit discussed earlier, that subterranean, amorphous form existing below the borders of both the US and Canada, and how it might be likened in a half-imagined, approachable and instructive pamphlet published by ConocoPhillips—entitled, say, *Drilling for Dummies*—to a coconut possessed by both the United States and Canada;

27.6/240) a continuation of the coconut analogy. Both the US and Canada are each horizontally inserting a straw into the husk of the one coconut to extract the coconut innards. The problem is that most of the volume of the coconut is trapped in the coconut meat, such that, through the processes of hydraulically fracturing the meat, both Canada and the US fill their cheeks with water and forcefully blow all that water into the coconut so that the water permeates the coconut meat and mixes with the coconut milk. This mixture is subsequently sucked back out and spit into a glass, where the rich milk and water is separated;

27.7/241) the relevant question. Exactly how much coconut is there? The USGS speculates that there are at least 7.4 billion barrels of coconut oil, 6.7 trillion cubic feet of natural coconut gas and 530 million barrels of *liquefied* natural coconut gas to be extracted. That's a lot of ice cream topping, a lot of frosting on a coconut cake;

27.8/242) a related question: how many folks with how many straws are actively at work trying to suck up all the coconut milk? Answer: more than six thousand. But as the Manitoba side of the coconut is largely inaccessible because of the unstable Brokton-Froid Fault zone (don't want to be sticking a straw in there!) and the Saskatchewan exposure is only a meager little tip, the overwhelming majority of productive coconut drilling and subsequent infrastructure occurs Stateside;

27.9/243) the fact that Canada is allowed access to the coconut below their border—*why* and exactly *what* agreements were made to give up the advantage of being sole-sipper and the repercussions resulting therefrom to be discussed in sum at another time. An analogous allusion to the Canadian mother-in-law that's haunted these pages elsewhere. Obese upon her arrival, seeming to have slipped down across the border like a foul weather front, hovering over everyone in that family, draped in her leafy green moo-moo, resembling thusly a carnivorous plant—a Venus Flytrap, for instance—growing resplendent in the space that she was invading, cooing, with overt exaggeration, in the face of America's future generation, who herself is much too old to be cooed at, enfolding the lithe teenager in her broad, polyester fronds, all the while complaining about her gout;

27.10/244) if not exactly like a weather front, then Canada likened to a lush mangrove island, who, after breaking away from the Canadian mangrove stand, becomes a leafy green clump floating slowly southward to dry up, whither and die;

27.11/245) a depiction of the Resident Alien first appearing in a holiday mood, ordering the acquisition of ingredients to formulate The Bloody Cesar [v + C (t + c) + T + W, where v = vodka, C = Clamato juice (itself comprised of (t) tomato juice and (c) clam broth), T = Tobasco Sauce and W = Worcestershire], Canada's national cocktail—*cheers!*—it's national *drink*. Served over ice, glass rimmed with celery salt, garnished with celery stalk and lime. Kicked back to salute a summer's worth of sunsets, and by the fall, looking northwestward, veritably dropping her glass and collapsing face-forward onto the back deck and into her coma;

28.1/246) a blizzard on the night of the doctor's mother's death. Visibility ranging from ten feet past the windshield to a quarter of a mile. Winds gusting to 42 miles per hour. Snowfall variable, ½ to 3 inches per hour, conditions exacerbated by groundblow. Crews working late afternoon through the overnight to keep the 25 miles of Rural Route 5 open to the Highway 85 North/South interchange;

28.2/247) just one day prior, a replacement's arrival, up from Sioux Falls, affording the doctor a week off, the Turtle Mountain Reservation Covid-19 outbreak still raging at the clinic, the entire family therefore wearing masks in the home, keeping their distance from one another (even the father and daughter, just to be fair), an attempt to prevent transmission that excludes the doctor's mother, of course, because what's the point, like really, *what's the point*? Her mother already so close to death, what's to shield her from, what's to protect her from? She can not be protected. She is finally in the very late stages of dying. Still, all surfaces scrubbed and rescrubbed, the doctor taking her meals in the kitchen alone so that she can remove her mask to eat;

28.3/248) a portrait of the doctor and her daughter sitting vigil. Three generations of women experiencing what must have been the most momentous occasion of their lives to date. The granddaughter reportedly sitting in a recliner brought in from the living room. The doctor herself up and roaming, no doubt lithely inspecting tubes and drips and readings on various dashboards, consoles and LED screens;

28.4/249) an uncommonly loud, rasping breath, like a succession of sighs born from some major aggravation, reportedly;

28.5/250) the small television on the dresser broadcasting the Hallmark Channel. The TV having been broadcasting the Hallmark Channel 24 hours, seven days a week for nearly four months now, starting a few days after the mother slipped into her coma. Programming on the restoration of love. Programming on the redemptive power of empathy. Programming on hope and kindness and courtesy. Targeted commercials for Pillsbury Rolls and Tylenol, fabric softeners and all forms of dairy products;

28.6/251) something hugely important happening in that bedroom. Everything momentous. The teenage daughter watching her mother, the doctor watching her mother, as her own mother experienced her death, a great blizzard of neurons going dark, one by one. Could she experience it, the doctor's mother, properly speaking, given the morphine, the cocktail of palliative drugs? The snow outside falling, covering the roads as quickly as they're plowed;

28.7/252) the snow lashing the window, a white rectangle, beyond which nothing else exists. But then of course a world exists out there, shrouded, at least temporarily, by the white blankness;

28.8/253) a question: doctor's daughter doing what?;

28.9/254) a question: doctor doing what?;

28.10/255) a question: doctor's mother doing what? A canvas disassembling back to blankness, accompanied, one could imagine, as the doctor herself might have requested, the violent "storm" movement in Vivaldi's otherwise heroic *Spring*, adopted for the recorder;

29.1/256) associations of death, predation, pollution and water made even more evident through discussion of the 1999 Arbitration Claim made under Chapter 11 bankruptcy by Sun Belt Water, Inc. (Santa Barbara, California), claiming $105 million dollars as a result of Canada's prohibition on the export of bulk water by marine tanker, eventually resulting in the dissolution of the Sun Belt Water corporation and its collateral interests;

29.2/257) Alberta, where so much of the water under discussion originates, weaponizing the *North-west Irrigation Act* (1894), the *Natural Resources Transfer Agreement* (1930), *The Framework of Water Rights Legislation in Canada* (1988) in its successful dissolution to all riparian claims to the Crown's "commoditization and ownership of nearly all waters" (Laidlaw and Passelac-Ross) used for drinking, swimming, farming, cooking, cleaning, livestock husbandry and "tailing ponds," described as depository of water used in the process of petroleum extrusion from the "Oil Sands," those enormous, man-made lakes—rather, the water contained therein—made so polluted that cannons are regularly fired over their surfaces in order to re-rout migrating birds, a deterrent that is unusually effective, except in the notable case when 1,600 ducks died after landing in a tailing pond outside of Fort McMurray (Canada), operated by Syncrude (2008);

29.3/258) the six thousand fracking wells previously referenced in *Drilling for Dummies* requiring approximately 5 billion gallons of fresh water to operate. Water that the Canadians provide from their geographically proximate Canadian fresh water sources. In exchange, they are permitted to operate on US soil;

29.4/259) the flowback—what flows back after the water is injected—containing toxic metals and brine and radioactive material. This they leave behind. Mostly it ends up in abandoned quarries excavated and ultimately abandoned from various strip mining operations due south;

29.5/260) water in nearby St. John township deemed potable despite the faint smell of sulfur. Farmland sold off in regions around St. John due to shortages in irrigation water. The Freyman Municipal "Swim Area," not a pool *per se*, but a large, clay bottomed depression with a wood island at its center for low-dive diving boards, remaining empty for the past two summers—swimming lessons canceled on short notice the first year, some nine months before the start of the pandemic;

29.6/261) the water in the "Swim Area," and the water from the aquifer that historically used to supply it, deemed unsafe. The question is how, on a sweltering Memorial Day, after a teenage girl spent a frustrated and overheated half-hour smearing Vaseline on a tampon just to "get it in" because all she wanted to do was go swimming—how, when she was standing there in her sandals and summer dress, the straps of her bikini drawn tight against her clavicles, pool bag complete with towel and goggles and sunblock and water bottle and strawberries in a Tupperware: just how to explain it to her? That the pool's closed for the summer? That there's no water? That, correction, there's water, sure, but it's not, like, *water*;

Chpt 30:
Economies of Desire

30.1/262) this question, albeit a rhetorical one. In as much as the Canadian experience can't be spoken for on the topic, is there a more sexualized field in the United States of America than the schoolyard during morning drop-off? The mothers' hair pulled back in frowzy ponytails or hidden snuggly beneath winter hats, the father wearing a wool watchman cap, fringe of greasy, unwashed hair fanning out the sides and off the nape of the neck. Everyone still stunned by the clock's alarm, the noisy marshaling of kids through breakfast, changes of clothes, morning toiletries, the finding and donning of masks;

30.2/263) a description of the sound of the buzzer beckoning the children—K through 12— into school, and how the parents just stand here, still warm from their beds, defenseless yet, as the day's just begun. The women without make-up, the man unshaven. There's an intimacy here, a collective intimacy born of the proximity of each other's natural bodies in their most natural state, post-repose. They seem to eye one another with absolute acceptance, as if to say of course we are here together, trusting each other in our defenselessness, despite the masks, our nakedness. Fully alive for a moment, a moment not defined by a shared material experience, that community of things, but its opposite;

30.3/264) all the things reduced to a red, uncovered Webber grill rusting in the rain on a deck in the cold, solemn, North Dakota night;

30.4/265) all the parents inevitably arriving back to their homes, back to their more stable domestic milieus, where even more intimate surprises—one might even call them *dramatic* surprises—occasionally occur. A husband might discover his wife lying naked on a carpet, for example, between the bed and sliding glass door that leads onto the patio from their bedroom. Maskless. Eyes open, staring at the ceiling. The husband, obviously concerned, calls to her from across the room, asking her what's going on, what's the matter here, what's happened here, why's she's like *this*?

30.5/266) an answer to the question why the wife is like this, naked on the floor, her beautiful porcelain skin, her lithe body curled up (she's lost too much weight, he notices), an image that he's maybe seen in a painting, the husband thinks, noting also for the first time the amount of acne that has appeared around her mouth and chin, a rash of small pimples. This is the closest he's been to her in months. "Come here and fuck me," she says. She has never, ever spoken that phrase, said those exact words in this exact order, not once, not ever;

30.6/267) a pause here. The husband takes three steps into the room, squats, stretches out his arms, places one hand on her hip, the other tracing his fingers across her back. He can't think of a way to respond. He feels hopelessly confused, utterly baffled as to what to do next, the whirring blizzard of sparks in his brain crackling, a primal fear rising. "Lay next to me," she says. He thinks the word "transmission." He thinks "daughter." He thinks about the things she said about how things had to be until this is all over. She hasn't been home for fourteen days yet, the window for symptoms to appear. Won't be, either. She'll be going back day after tomorrow, back to the whole infected horde. Is it this fact that has her in the state he now finds her? Is this an expression of her grief for her mother's death? Both? Does she need to be taken to a hospital? What hospital? Where? Suddenly he feels to need to run. He needs to go for a run. He can feel the hot, irrational fear of panic burning through the benzo he took at breakfast. He manages to say: "Maybe let's just think about this for a second." He says, "Maybe I should go for a run";

30.7/268) the naked wife in the patch of sun on the rug now sobbing. The husband, continuing to cup her hip, tracing her spine with his fingertips. "Is it worth it?" she asks, "*this*?" "You tell me," he says. " Jesus Christ," she says, "you don't even *run*." "Not true," the husband says, then rises, rummages through the dresser at the foot of the bed, puts together the articles of clothing of what he believes approximates something one could functionally run in, says "Love you," and leaves. He opens the front door and steps out into the world where this same thing must be happening all the time, all over the place;

31.1/269) Powel's and Snellman's definition of the "knowledge economy as production and services based on knowledge-intensive activities that contribute to an accelerated pace of technical and scientific advance, as well as rapid obsolescence. The key component of a knowledge economy is a greater reliance on intellectual capabilities than on physical inputs or natural recourses";

31.2/270) an emphasis put on the phrase "rapid obsolescence" above;

31.3/271) Finland!;

31.4/272) a Pictogram Graph, in Finish flag navy blue and white, depicting how Finland's economy in the 1960s was based almost exclusively on paper production and forestry;

31.5/273) evidence of the seismic shift between skilled and unskilled labor in broad shouldered silhouettes, sometimes cleaved in half, sometimes quartered pictographic figures, themselves orange on white background;

31.6/274) orange, hard-hatted workers representing patent applications: the instantaneous visual transmission of Finish patents for telecommunications in 2000 (51.5%), compared to 1990 patent applications (8.9%). Paper and pulp patents plummeting in the decade referenced. Lots of halved and quartered hard-hatted, orange workers here;

31.7/275) unanimous consensus amongst economists in general that, obviously, technological advancement has significantly increased the demand for highly skilled labor at the expense of low-skilled labor;

31.8/276) a crazy, out of the blue thought, speaking of knowledge acquisition, premised on the inevitable sale of Geronimo Joe's. Did he even hold a note on that dump, or did he own it outright? If the latter, wait until it comes up for auction. Could even keep the name, the whole thing to be had no doubt for next to nothing. A reminder to research comparables, if any comparables can even be found;

31.9/277) a return to Epstein's recent argument that, not so obviously, generalists, rather than specialists, are more viable agents of production in the knowledge economy. This because he makes a distinction between what he terms "wicked" and "kind" environments. Navigating a wicked environment puts a premium on the generalist's adaptability, those who are able to navigate ambiguity and reconcile one's self to the "opacity of abstraction" (Tanner). In other words, one needs to be able to be at home in the real world. A kind environment, on the other hand, within which specialists thrive, is one typified by clear rules and goals and outcomes, as well as the certainty of repetition, and accurate and immediate feedback;

310.9/278) examples put forth of generalists: human resource managers, psychotherapists, quality control, forestry;

31.11/279) examples put forth of specialists: golfers, psy-
chiatrists, chess players, a musician who, having scrubbed
three of John Adson's (1587-1640) *Courtly Masquing Ayres*
of the recorder (or "blockfloten") using her Garage Band
app, is able to pipe away with the remaining flutes, oboes
and strings when blasted through her I-Phone speaker;

31.12/280) a following of Epstein's line of reasoning to
its logical terminus. The promotion of the generalist disposition in the wicked (i.e., real) world requires, at times,
the removal of the golf clubs, the insistence on seeing the
whole person rather than the discreet, constituent parts
of the person, the clearing of the chess board, the hiding
of the recorder(s) on the top shelf of the master bedroom
closet, shrouded in a pillowcase, buried deeper than when
first hid here before, now sandwiched in four seasons of
bedding, and a prophylactically-prepared response to their
missing: where are they, her recorders (the Ginzu knife-like
roll of instruments)? Has anyone *seen* them? Did she leave
them in her locker? Are they in the car? At school? Did she
check the lost and found?;

31.13/281) the admonishment that everyone around here
better start taking better care of their things;

CHPT 32:
CONCLUSIONS

32.1/282) a suspension in space, a looking down at a muddy gravel road. Across the road, a fieldstone ranch-style home. In the background, a woman situated approximately eleven feet downwind and to the left of the front door, butt in the air, a strip of bare, white skin visible between the waist of her jeans and heavy sweater, head in an ornamental evergreen, apparently pruning, taking advantage of a truly weird, almost unprecedented mid-January thaw. A teenaged girl sitting on the stoop in an unbuttoned peacoat, her knees knocked together, the top of her head visible, but not her face, as she's looking down at her smartphone. Some twenty-five feet in the foreground, upwind of everyone, a man standing where the home's walkway merges at a T with the municipal sidewalk, dressed in a baggy hoodie and cargo pants. In his right hand, a rainbow colored, braided leash. At the end of the leash, a matching braided collar buckled around the neck of a dog;

32.2/283) a late model Hyundia Santa Fe entering from the right, stopping in front the house, obscuring the view of the man and the dog;

32.3/284) a young woman of athletic build appearing at the rear of the vehicle (who's in the driver's seat?) wearing Lycra exercise tights and a form-fitting pink fleece jacket. She reaches into her jacket pocket, removes a pink mask, puts it on. The man reaches into the thigh pocket of his cargo pants, removes a red bandana, ties it around his face;

32.4/285) the opening of the Hyundia's cargo hatch;

32.5/286) the man reappearing at the back of the SUV with the dog, keeping a good distance between himself and the woman. An exchange of quickly forgotten pleasantries;

32.6/287) the dog, wagging its tail. The same dog that pissed on the carpets. The same dog that shat on two bedroom floors, as well as in the kitchen and foyer. The dog that chewed the tongue of one of the man's $130 Merrill snow boots. The dog that barfed on a favorite West Elm rug. The same dog that didn't know how to stay or come or heel. Who jumped on people, family members and visitors alike, and wouldn't stop jumping. Who made the man abject. The dog an unforgivable failure of the family. Couldn't they even raise a dog right?;

32.7/288) not a conclusion at all, but the acceptance of a total and totalizing indictment;

32.8/289) the daughter forced to be here, to bear witness;

32.9/290) the woman in the pink fleece standing in the muddy road (in the dirty glut of the thaw), rapping on the floor of the cargo area of her SUV with the palm of her hand. The dog looking at her, then at the man, wagging its tail;

32.10/291) the man commanding *up* and the dog wagging its tail, just standing there, looking up;

32.11/292) the man yelling "up" again and the dog just standing there, looking up at the man;

32.12/293) the man bending down and lifting the dog up, the woman in the fleece giving him acceptably wide berth, and his setting the dog in the cargo area. The dog wagging his tail;

32.13/294) the man stepping back until the rainbow col-ored leash is taut, the woman stepping in his place, un-clasping the tether, the leash itself falling limply onto the muddy road, the man, not knowing what else to do, coiling it, tapping the muddy leash on his thigh;

32.14/295) the woman in the pink fleece peering into the back and shutting the hatch. She offers her hand to the man, quickly withdrawing it, no doubt a force of habit, his-toric sign that the exchange of goods and/or services has been consummated;

32.15/296) the woman disappearing again behind the truck, and then the truck pulling away, leaving the man standing in the road in front of the house;

32.16/297) the teenage girl standing up from the stoop and walking into the house;

32.17/298) the woman with her head in the bush to the left of the door that the girl closes still pruning the ornamental evergreen. Or is she adjusting the mulch? Whatever. She'll be gone again tomorrow;

32.18/299) the man turning his head to the right, presumably following the departure of the truck. He is slapping his thigh with the empty leash;

32.19/300) the man turning his head to the left again, in this direction. He is getting smaller and smaller;

32.20/301) the house, getting smaller and smaller;

32.21/302) the man keeping track of all of this, keeping his eye on things even now, looking in this direction;

32.22/303) off in the near distance, the blur of a landscape behind him: Canada.

CHRISTOPHER GRIMES lives with his wife, daughter and dog in the Chicago area.